I walked along the path past other plots, some well-tended and some overgrown, past the tall stalks and empty heads of sunflowers, the various composting methods people had devised, the thick hedges of raspberries and the twining stems of grapevines.

The path grew crowded, blocked by people, who glanced at me and moved away until I could see into the center of it. The noise of busy whispering filled the air like a swarm of bees.

Straight ahead, Lois knelt in the dirt of her garden plot beside a trench she'd been digging, her hands pressed to her chest. The trench so carefully emptied of dirt was instead full of a tumble of pale flesh and spandex and brassy blond hair. . . .

By Lora Roberts
*Published by Fawcett Books:*

MURDER IN A NICE NEIGHBORHOOD
MURDER IN THE MARKETPLACE
MURDER MILE HIGH
MURDER BONE BY BONE
MURDER CROPS UP

# MURDER CROPS UP

## Lora Roberts

FAWCETT GOLD MEDAL • NEW YORK

A Fawcett Gold Medal Book
Published by The Ballantine Publishing Group
Copyright © 1998 by Lora Roberts Smith

http://www.randomhouse.com

Library of Congress Catalog Card Number: 97-95364

ISBN 0-449-15048-8

Manufactured in the United States of America

First Edition: September 1998

10  9  8  7  6  5  4  3  2  1

For the menfolks

This book is set in one of Palo Alto's community gardens, but no other similarity exists between real life and this work of fiction. No real people were harmed in the making of this book, since none of the characters are based on real people or resemble them in any way. (Hint: Real people don't behave in a work of fiction. They want to go their own way. So I don't allow them in.)

The actual community gardeners are just what you'd expect of gardeners—unassuming, nurturing, helpful to each other, and content to be left alone with their patch of earth and their seedlings. I thank them very much for the loan of their garden, and hope I give it back to them without the loss of one earthworm.

# 1 _____

I was eating a Tompkins King apple and admiring my article about winter-blooming hellebores in the latest issue of *Organic Gardening* when Lois Humphries came to visit me the first time.

I didn't realize, when I saw her make her way down the driveway to where I sat on the front porch steps, soaking up the unseasonable warmth of a sunny mid-November afternoon, that her visit would precipitate a whole load of trouble on my head. I thought the worst thing on my horizon was the absence of Paul Drake, the Palo Alto police detective who owns the house in front of mine. Lois gave his house a glance as she went past it, and I could see her mentally comparing his larger, professionally painted bungalow with my rickety cottage.

She saw me sitting on the porch and let herself in through the gate that divides my portion of the driveway from Drake's. I shut the magazine, keeping one finger in to save my place, and set down my apple core.

"Hello, Liz. So this is where you live?"

"This is it." I regarded her with misgiving. At the community garden where I had a plot, Lois was the person who volunteered for jobs requiring a talent for bossiness and a thick skin, since other gardeners inevitably resented being bossed. Her presence on my doorstep could only signal that she'd figured out I wasn't doing my share, and she had a plan to fix that. "To what do I owe the pleasure of this visit?"

"I just hope you'll consider it a pleasure when I tell you why I've come," she said ominously, pinching her lips together at the end of the sentence, as she always did. She was a thin woman, somewhere between sixty and seventy. Her hair was thin, her lips were thin, and I suspected her mind had no extraordinary width either.

"Well, why don't you tell me?" I stood up. "Would you like to come in?"

My dog, Barker, was eager for her to come in, judging from the whines and barks that came from inside the front door. Barker had been out with me earlier, frisking through shafts of sunlight, harrying squirrels up the redwood trees. Then, unable to resist a cat washing her nether regions on the sidewalk in front of Drake's house, he'd jumped the fence for a closer look. I'd put him inside as punishment.

Lois looked at the door apprehensively. "No, thanks. Your dog sounds dangerous."

"Oh, he is." I took wicked pleasure in fostering Barker's image as a rough, tough doggie. He is big, black and white, and rambunctious, but the danger he poses to most people is the usual canine fault of injudicious sniffing.

"We can handle this out here." Lois withdrew a clipboard from her big bag. "As you know, the work day is tomorrow."

"I got the garden newsletter. And I saw that you've volunteered to organize the gardeners to do maintenance jobs."

"That's right. I would have called you," Lois continued, "but your phone number isn't listed in the community garden roster." She held a pen, poised over her clipboard, ready to write down my number.

"I don't have a phone."

"Don't have a phone!" Lois found this too incredible to believe. "No one can exist without a telephone."

"I can." I didn't tell her that I did have access to a phone. Drake lets me receive messages at his number, which I've given to all the magazine editors who might want to get in touch with me. Maybe it's a little cumbersome, but I like it. "What did you want to tell me?"

Lois sniffed. "I just wanted to make sure you'll be at the work day tomorrow."

"I planned to come. Do you need volunteers so badly you go looking for them?"

"I wouldn't have to beat the bushes if Rita would just bestir herself," Lois retorted. "She thinks everything will go smoothly without any organization. I don't know what the city pays her for."

"They don't pay her much." I knew how much the garden coordinator made because I'd thought of applying for the job when it fell vacant shortly after I'd become a community gardener a few years ago. At that time I didn't have a fixed residence; in fact, I lived in my VW bus. And by the time I'd become a homeowner, the job had been filled by a peppy young woman named Rita Dancey, who was pleasant and enthusiastic on the rare occasions we saw her at the garden.

"She took the job, so she should do it." Lois drew herself up. "And instead, I have to spend my time making sure enough people come to get the work done."

3

"Well, I'll be there in the morning." The garden had provided me with a good portion of my sustenance during the years I lived in Palo Alto in my bus. I hadn't really given back what that was worth. I didn't go to meetings or potlucks, rarely showed up at work days. I weeded the paths around my plot and kept it neat, but I felt guilty over my lack of communal participation. Thing is, I'm just not a potluck, all-one-happy-family kind of person.

"You haven't shown up in the past. I want to make sure that gardeners who haven't been helping out join us to do their share." Lois always spoke with the firm assurance of those who know they are right, but there was an extra measure of satisfaction in her voice.

"I've said I'll come."

"I'm sure you will, Liz." She smiled at me in triumph, as if she felt power over me. "People who don't attend might get talked about. And if people started talking about you—well, I have it on the best authority that there'd be plenty to talk about."

Astounded, I stared at her. For a moment she looked uneasy, then she pinned her firm smile back into place. "So be sure to get there early," she instructed. "I have a very special job for you to do."

She turned around and marched back up the driveway, through the gate that closed off my yard from Drake's. Behind me, Barker escalated his whining, anxious to get his nose into the visitor's crotch before it was too late. By the time I thought about letting him out, Lois had gotten all the way up the drive.

I sat back down, but I couldn't recapture the simple pleasure I'd felt before Lois's visit. If her purpose had been to make me feel paranoid, she had succeeded. Because she was right. For one reason or another, there was plenty to gossip about where I was concerned.

I carried the *Organic Gardening* into the house without glancing again at my byline. I put the apple core in the compost bucket. My kitchen, immaculately clean, with the blue glass bowl I'd found at a yard sale for a dollar catching the last amber rays of sunlight, didn't cheer me as it usually did.

In the living room, I put the magazine into a clippings file in my desk, which occupies one corner of the small room. A couch sits at a right angle to the fireplace, with a comfy chair across from it, next to a small table stacked just then with library books.

It still gave me a thrill to look at that chair and realize that I could sit there that evening, a lamp turned on to give light to my page, and read until I was sleepy, whenever that was, and go to bed in a real bed, and get up to make breakfast in a real kitchen. I had had all these amenities for a year now, but I never took them for granted. Living in the bus had taught me a lot about simplicity, about traveling light. But I wasn't sorry to have moved inside.

The only thing I'd been sorry about, before Lois came by, was Drake's absence. I had taken him to the airport the day before. His father had been stricken out of the blue with aplastic anemia, and Drake was needed not just as a son, but also as a potential blood and bone marrow donor. All day, the sight of his ancient Saab parked in the space behind his house had given me a sense of dislocation—it was Friday, Drake should have been at work, but his car was home and he was in Seattle. I had had difficulty settling and had accomplished little all day, and then the mail had brought me the always-welcome experience of seeing myself in print, and for a time I'd forgotten that I wouldn't be seeing Drake that evening.

We were good friends as well as neighbors, but our relationship had been changing in the past few months. In fact, just thinking of it as a relationship was a major step for me; my first impulse is to back away from any emotional tie or commitment. Drake was changing that—he was changing me, whether I wanted to change or not.

Now I missed him more than I wanted to. As well, I felt a certain amount of relief at the interruption of his relentless courtship. I meant to take a clear look at what was developing between us, and see if it was something I wanted.

Barker dogged my footsteps through the house until I dished up his nightly portion of Active Chow. My chow took the form of a baked potato, topped with garlic chives and parsley from the raised beds in my yard, and the added luxury of grated cheddar and plain yogurt. I brought my current book, Charlotte Brontë's *Shirley*, to the table with me.

For once fiction couldn't take me away. Instead, my mind began turning over Lois's words, wondering what lay behind them.

The whole incident had seemed unlike her. Lois was sometimes abrasive, but she didn't usually resort to underhanded methods like blackmail to get her way. She had been told, she'd said, that there was plenty to talk about regarding me.

I didn't think of myself as a fascinating topic of conversation—a woman in my mid-thirties, living frugally and quietly with no telephone, no TV, who kept to myself and liked it that way. However, I had more than once been involved in violent death, through no fault of my own.

It was that, I supposed, to which Lois referred. Other gardeners might not want someone around who is known to have lived in her car for a time, to have been suspected of murdering a dear old lady who was her benefactor, and then to have encountered murder again, not that long ago.

I could only hope that my tidy garden, my weed-free path, spoke up for me. I hoped that people engaged in the common task of nurturing and sustaining would have no inclination for sensational gossip.

Lois, though, was prepared to believe the worst about me, and to make everyone else at the garden do so, too, unless I did as I was told. And that was what I couldn't figure out. If she'd denounced me at a committee meeting, got me booted out, it would be more like her steamroller approach to issues. What had made her decide to use the threat of making me notorious to twist my arm? Perhaps the same someone who'd filled her in on my sins had put her up to using them against me.

I finished my baked potato, no wiser than I'd been when I'd started eating. I cleaned up the kitchen and then was free to build a fire, using logs I'd dragged home from downed trees along San Francisquito Creek. I watched the green flames for a little while before going back to *Shirley*.

I couldn't concentrate on the travails of the Luddites, no matter how much I sympathized with them. I kept thinking of the garden, always before a refuge for me, a place of almost sacred importance. I didn't know all the gardeners, just the ones whose plots ranged with mine.

Though they had their quirks, I couldn't imagine any of them stooping to petty intimidation.

Who, among those gentle, plant-nurturing people, had it in for me? I wanted to know, and I meant to find out.

# 2

**THE** community garden behind Palo Alto's main library was usually a cheerful place. Spread out on a few acres near the library, the haphazard patchwork of garden plots had a rustic charm, punctuated by withered cornstalks and the purple heads of unpicked artichokes. Silvery fava beans pushed up through rich brown soil. The ancient smell of vegetative mold filled the air, effectively blocking the exhaust fumes of traffic on Embarcadero Road.

But although the garden looked mellow, the vibes were anything but. The cool air didn't seem very fresh. People formed small clumps, talking in undertones instead of mulching their paths and fixing the fence that encircled the site.

I put down the posthole digger and pushed back my hat—a gaudy flowered straw that had been marked down at the Thrift Mart to $1.98, well within my meager budget. The bandanna I wiped my face with was also a Thrift Mart special, old and soft and comfortable from my first day of possessing it. I took off the hat and wiped my forehead, too. Despite the temperature, I was sweating.

"Hey, Liz!" Bridget Montrose waved at me and charged in my direction, her youngest child tucked under her arm for quick movement. Moira didn't particularly like that. She wanted to be down, exploring on her sturdy toddler legs. "I hoped I'd see you here."

I put my hat back on and smiled at Bridget, who radiated normality in the thick atmosphere. "Hey, Biddy. I went by your house on my way here, but no one was home. I was going to offer you a ride over."

Bridget grinned. She had dressed for the work day in old sweatpants that made no secret of her ample hips, and an Addison Elementary School sweatshirt so covered with paint stains that its original blue was visible only in stripes. Moira was far more chic in cute kiddie overalls— much cuter than the adult version I wore—and a ruffled T-shirt. The only girl in a family of rambunctious boys, Moira got ruffles from every direction.

"Corky had a soccer game at eight this morning. After that, I went by your house." She blushed a little. "I peeked in your garage window and saw your gardening tools were gone, so I guessed you'd come here. That's when I remembered about the work day." Bridget glanced around and lowered her voice. "I'm just putting in an appearance. Sam's at a karate tournament, and there's also a work day at Mick's preschool. Emery is tearing out his hair trying to figure out how to do it all. I've got to get back to help him out."

Lois came bustling up, her eyes full of that strange, hard triumph. "You aren't finished already, are you, Liz? Nice to see you at one of our work days, Bridget." She gave Bridget a Look that said as plainly as words that she was usually more conspicuous by her absence than her presence.

I wielded the posthole digger for one more scoop. Lois had met me at the gate that morning with the digger and the job of putting in a row of postholes on the west side of the garden, near the main gate. "Seven holes doesn't look like a lot," I said, catching my breath. "But they're hard to dig."

Lois walked over to one. "This isn't nearly deep enough." Her firm voice brooked no back talk. "They need to go down at least three feet." She walked on down the line of the fence, checking out the other holes I'd dug.

"You really got a bad assignment here," Bridget whispered, keeping one eye on Lois. "Does she have it in for you, or what?"

"Who knows?" I stuffed the bandanna back in my pocket. "Why were you looking for me?"

"Hmm? Oh, Claudia's birthday. I've been meaning to plan something, and now it's really getting late."

"When is Claudia's birthday? I didn't know she had one. Thought she sprang out of the earth, fully formed, like the other goddesses."

Bridget laughed. "She has a birthday. Just doesn't want anyone to make a fuss. But I'm going to. Make a fuss, I mean. After all, it's not every day a woman turns sixty." She frowned at me. "Now Lois is going to stick me with some job or other that will take a while, and Emery will be mad. If you had a telephone, this would never have happened." She broke off her tirade and looked at me closely. "What? What did I say?"

I pulled my face together, not wanting my expression to show so clearly what I was thinking. For years my survival had depended on keeping a poker face, revealing nothing of my inner life on the surface. It wasn't good to let my guard slip, let myself be so easily read.

"I just get tired of being picked on for not having a phone," I said, when it became clear that Bridget would

11

wait forever if necessary for me to answer her. "Lois already tore a strip off me for that."

Bridget frowned. "She didn't call to remind me."

Moira squatted down to sift through the dirt I'd dug. She squealed with delight when she found a worm. Watching her, I drew in a few breaths of the crisp fall air, and tried to tell myself that it was all my imagination—the dark miasma that seemed to fill the air, the sense of being whispered about, the looks that evaporated when I met them. Just being treated normally by Bridget went a long way to allay the paranoia Lois had roused in me the previous day, and which seemed to have reached full flower that morning.

All the same, I knew it wasn't my imagination. Just because you're paranoid doesn't mean that people aren't talking about you.

I willed myself to shake it off. I looked up at the pale wash of sky, at the dark red branches of the Japanese plum trees that marched around the garden on the other side of the perimeter path. The trees shifted gently in the wind, their falling leaves animating them. The bite of approaching winter flowed beneath the surface of the sun-warmed air, like the constant stir of dry leaves beneath the sounds of people working and talking.

I wanted back the sense of well-being I had grown used to over the past few months, the feeling that it was good to be alive, instead of just surprising.

Californians pay attention to karma, to the meddling of fate in their lives. I was just waiting for fate to decide not to pick on me anymore.

Lois came back from her inspection. "Those postholes all need to be at least a foot deeper," she said, her sharp nose quivering with displeasure. Beneath her shady straw hat, locks of gray hair straggled around her face. She pulled off her sunglasses and let them dangle around her neck by a cord. A single clear drop at the end of her nose succumbed to the tissue she dabbed at it, then slowly collected again. She gave it another swipe while she surveyed Bridget and then stared at Moira.

"Didn't you get the flyer, Bridget? I asked that parents only bring children old enough to be helpful."

"Moira's helping," Bridget insisted stoutly. "She's disposing of snails."

Moira opened her grimy paw and held it up to Lois, her smile beatific. A snail made a slow, desperate break for it across her palm. Before it could escape, she closed the prison door again.

Lois recoiled in horror. "Don't you know snails carry viruses? I never touch them with my bare skin."

"Lucky snails," Bridget muttered, not loud enough for Lois to hear her. Struggling with a smile, I felt better.

"Well, it's none of my business anyway," Lois said, pinching her lips together. "I just came over to thank you for coming to the work day, and remind you to sign the petition."

"What petition?" Bridget looked puzzled.

"Really, Bridget." Lois pounced on this evidence of flightiness. "I outlined it in the flyer I sent out. The petition about the low-income housing and the library."

"Well, I'm certainly for those things."

Lois stiffened.

"Um, Biddy—" I tried to warn Bridget, but she kept talking, certain I was on her side.

"You know how it is around here now, Liz." She turned to me. "Our neighborhood is getting filled up with

Beamers and Mercedeses. The houses cost so much, nobody with children can afford to buy them. Corky's best friend moved away last year, and we got a two-income couple who are never home. Not much contribution to the neighborhood there."

Lois's face slowly turned as purple as the leaves of the plum trees. "The petition is against a plan to put that housing here, right on top of our gardens!"

"Oh." Bridget blinked. "I didn't know about that. When did they decide to do that?"

"They haven't." I could see that Lois was too full of indignation to talk, so I filled Bridget in. "Evidently the city has the garden down as a possible housing site, or as a place to expand the library. The petition is to ask them to remove the garden from their use inventory and dedicate it as community agricultural, or some such thing."

"I see." Bridget nodded. "I do remember hearing something about that before." She looked around. "It would be a shame to put houses here where we've worked so hard."

"Exactly." Lois allowed her thin lips to smile. "You can see how important it is that every gardener sign."

"I know you want me to, Lois," Bridget said apologetically. "But I have to think about it. I love the garden, and it's an important resource, but people are more important. Palo Alto needs some affordable housing."

"You—have to think about it?" Lois's jaw dropped open.

"Yes. I might not sign." Bridget picked up Moira, who was trying to insert her small body into the hole I'd dug.

"You—might not sign." Outrage gathered on Lois's face.

I did the heroic thing and distracted her. "Are you sure the postholes aren't deep enough?" I tried to put a bit of whine in my voice, and succeeded all too admirably.

14

Lois vented her anger on me. "They certainly are not. You'll have to go down at least another foot in all of them. We want a fence that won't fall down this time. Do you know that all but one of my pumpkins was stolen last week?" She eyed me as if she suspected that I did know, and had the aforesaid pumpkins stashed in my VW bus right then. "All but one!"

Bridget put herself in the line of fire. She said innocently, "A stronger fence won't keep out people who want to plunder our plots. They can just climb over it, or come in through the gate."

"We are making it tall. Tall and very, very strong." Lois glared at her, then at me. "That's why the fence postholes need to be deep." She took a breath. "And I'm expecting each of you to sign that petition. This is very important to all of us, and we must present a united front." She wasn't finished yet. "As for your garden plot, Bridget, if you don't clean it up this fall and plant a cover crop—"

"Hello, fellow dirtbags!" The cheery voice came from Rita Dancey, the twentysomething part-time manager of the community gardens. She was her usual perky self, wearing a sports bra and cycling shorts despite the cool weather. She didn't really have the behind for cycling shorts, and a bulge of too, too solid flesh followed the bottom of the sports bra around her midsection, but I gave her an *E* for effort. Her blond hair bounced on top of her head, confined by a bright purple scrunchie and a soiled white visor advertising Pete's Wicked Ale. "Are we having fun yet?"

I wasn't. I didn't like Lois's nagging and shoving to get people to execute her agenda, but at least she was usually straightforward about it. Rita was so bouncy and cheerful, she set my teeth on edge. Although she talked a good game, she only showed up at the work days. The rest of the time she was out of there, not even returning telephone messages, according to some grumbling I'd heard. There were those who wondered what she did to earn her tiny salary. Looking at her now, I wondered if she was the person behind Lois, urging her to make people offers they couldn't refuse.

Lois pinched her lips together. "I was just explaining to Bridget that she needs to clean up her plot if she wants to retain the right to use it." She glared at Rita. "You are going to start enforcing the rules, aren't you? As we agreed at the last steering committee meeting? Gardeners who don't tidy their plots over the winter will forfeit them."

"Well, I wouldn't go that far." Rita turned to Bridget. "You're going to get your plot fixed up, right, Bridget? I wouldn't want to have to take it away."

"I'll do my best," Bridget said meekly.

"After all, you folks just love to grub in the dirt, don't you?" The unnerving thing about Rita, I decided, was that her expression didn't change. She was always smiling, sparkling, upbeat. There was something wrong with her, obviously.

"Whatcha up to here?" Her voice was loud and cheerful. "New fence postholes? Good work." She nudged the old chicken-wire fence, flat on the ground after being detached from its rusty metal posts. "This stuff is good for a little more time, huh? We recycle, right?"

Lois unpinched her lips to reply to that. "That wire is worse than useless. We're building a proper fence today." She glanced over at the pile of wood next to the Dumpster.

Rita followed the glance, and her gaze turned a little

steely. "This wasn't in the list of approved projects, Lois. You know we agreed—"

"I got all the lumber donated." Lois sounded aggrieved. "And what thanks do I get?"

"You couldn't possibly have gotten enough lumber donated to go all around the garden." Rita spoke with cold authority. "Certainly not in that little bitty pile there. That's barely enough to do a few feet on either side of the gate."

"It's enough to start with," Lois said stubbornly. Bridget and I looked at each other, and I could see we'd had the same thought. The fence postholes I'd dug fronted Lois's own garden, a few feet away from the gate. The new board fence would primarily benefit her. "And who made you such an expert, anyway?"

"My stepfather is in construction. I know how much wood it takes to build a fence." Rita looked at the postholes again. "I'm afraid you'll have to clear this with the committee, Lois. We haven't obtained the right permits for a new fence. If you want to repair the old one, go right ahead."

What she said was reasonable, but the tone of her voice made it clear that scores were being settled. She tossed her ponytail, gave us another of her wide, meaningless smiles, and bounced off.

Lois didn't say anything else, just pursed her lips angrily and stalked away down the bark-delineated path, stooping to yank up a hapless mallow plant that had the audacity to grow in her way.

"Whew." Bridget put Moira back down again. "Rita sure steamrolled Lois, didn't she? And Lois is really wearing her underwear too tight."

"She's been this way since her husband died last

17

summer." I took a swig from the water bottle I'd brought with me. "He kind of mellowed her out, I guess. Anyway, I've noticed that ever since then she goes around the garden finding fault with what people are doing. Like what she said about your garden."

Bridget looked worried. "I know my plot isn't very tidy, but it's not so bad, is it?"

"You've got Bermuda grass. There's nothing good about that." I shouldered the posthole diggers. "At least Rita has saved me from more of this. I'm going to put these over with the rest of the tools."

Bridget brightened. "And Lois didn't stick around long enough to give me a horrible job. I guess I'd better go fight the Bermuda grass for a while." She picked up Moira.

"I'll help you. We can talk about Claudia's party."

"Won't Lois be mad if you quit your job?"

I glanced over at the Dumpster. Lois had cornered Rita. The way they scowled at each other, it was clear they weren't having a friendly conversation.

"I think Lois is going to be busy being mad at someone else right now." I dumped the posthole digger on the pile of tools and followed Bridget down the path.

# 3

**BRIDGET** turned over the dirt with her shovel and I pulled out long, white roots of Bermuda grass. There was a lot of it, especially since her plot marched with the boundary fence on one side. Just outside the fence was a lush crop of the noxious weed.

"We really should dig all that up, too."

"Oh, please." Bridget pushed her shiny brown hair away from her face. "People are rabid about Bermuda grass around here. If I get it out of the paths and common areas, what difference does it make if it's in the garden bed? That's my problem, right?"

"Not according to Lois." I grabbed another handful of roots, stuffing them into a plastic five-gallon bucket, one of many I scrounged from construction sites. They were useful for everything from weed patrol to hauling compost from the city's periodic giveaway program. "She says that when you get a plot, you agree to keep it free from invasive weeds, like sow thistles and Bermuda grass." I added reluctantly, "She has a point, you know. This stuff has a long reach." I held up one of the foot-long underground stems; its fleshy segments were delineated by hairlike feeder roots, like tiny beards, at every joint. I was careful to pull the stem out of the ground gently, hoping to get the whole thing, not break it off and leave one of the segments to regrow.

"Yeah, yeah." Bridget went back to digging. "I don't know how people keep this stuff out of their gardens without digging full time, you know?" She pointed her shovel at the next-door garden before stomping it into the dirt again. "Like Webster Powell, for instance." She took another breather, glancing around the garden area. "Did he come to the work day? I notice he doesn't need to tidy his plot."

The resentment in her voice made me smile. Bridget is so easygoing, it's unusual when she lets loose with a complaint. "He can get on your nerves, for sure," I agreed, looking over the bender boards that divided Bridget's plot from Webster's. "He's probably the one complaining about your Bermuda grass. Not a speck to be seen in his garden."

"I see." Bridget leaned on her shovel, taking deep breaths. "Moira, don't put that in your mouth. Yes, he's even gotten rid of it outside the fence. Does that guy have a life?"

"I don't think so," I said, after due consideration. "He's here a lot, even on weekdays." I reached over and removed the tasty-looking grub from Moira's grasp, handing her a rounded pebble as a substitute. "Dirty. Don't eat it." Moira wanted the grub back, but I managed to squash it underfoot before she could figure out where it went. "Isn't he a software engineer? He has that nerd look."

"He's a consultant." Bridget abandoned her shovel and came to squat beside me, combing the long roots from the soil. "He's done some work for Emery, that's how I know about him. But he's not married, hardly dates or anything. I guess he must spend all his spare time here."

"Too bad he has to be next to you." I couldn't help but notice the contrast between the two plots.

Bridget's was still a haphazard mass of dead cornstalks, expiring tomato plants, and mildewed vines punctuated with bloated, yellow cucumbers. Webster had already cleared his raised beds; fava beans were a foot high in precise geometric formation on several of them, with one bed given over to winter greens. He had installed a big, lidded compost container, and had a large, shiny, new wheelbarrow padlocked to the fence post—a good precaution, since even my rusty, garage-sale wheelbarrow had recently rolled mysteriously away.

Not a blade of Bermuda grass, not an overlooked cluster of purslane or sow thistle, marred the perfection of Webster's garden. All the paths between his raised beds, as well as the one in front of his plot, were thickly mulched with wood chips from the mountain of them that the city had piled outside the garden fence.

We were silent for a moment, raking our gloved fingers through the soil and putting the endless supply of roots into the bucket. Bridget's soil was very nice, actually; she wasn't a tidy gardener, but she did throw in a lot of chicken manure and compost and rock dust whenever she planted, and the result was a dark, crumbly loam that contained many happy worms, to Moira's delight.

"I read somewhere that leaving the cornstalks and bean stalks up over the winter is good," Bridget said, rising and dusting the dirt off her knees. "I was going to try it, but I guess I'll just haul everything down and make everybody happy."

"Okay." I started pulling up the bean carcasses. "We

21

could break them up with our hands and dig them in, you know. That would be good, too."

"Let's." Bridget cheered up at this iconoclastic view. "So what if it doesn't make perfect beds." She cast a disparaging glance at Webster's garden. "His beds look like graves, anyway."

"Maybe he's got a few enemies buried there." The moment I said it, I wished it unsaid. Given recent events, I was afraid to make even a mild joke about death.

Bridget's thoughts, too, were driven in that direction. "Did you know that Melanie and Hugh are in counseling now?"

"No, I didn't." Melanie Dixon, along with birthday girl Claudia, was a member of a local writers' group that Bridget and I belonged to. The body that had been found recently under a sidewalk had ended up affecting Melanie's life; evidently her marriage was feeling the strain.

"At least they're working it out." Bridget took some rusty shears from her gardening basket and attacked a cornstalk. Moira, attracted by destruction, started pulling the withered leaves off the cornstalk and tossing them into the wind, laughing with delight, her little white pearls of teeth gleaming in her rosy mouth. Bridget smiled indulgently, her bad mood lightening. "I'm sure they'll get it together. I hate to think of families being torn apart by divorce."

"At least you know that won't happen to you." Bridget and Emery had a pretty solid marriage, it seemed to me. Of course, I don't know much about achieving success as a couple. My one experience with marriage had not been good, and I was shy of making another attempt at intimacy.

Once again, Bridget's thoughts paralleled mine. "So, are you missing Paul?"

"Not really." I stabbed a few bean stalks, getting my expression in order. "He's only been gone a couple of days."

"Have you heard from him? How's his dad?"

"He called last night."

"And you just happened to be there in his house?"

I could feel the color washing my face. "We arranged before he left that he would call at eight each night if he could. I go over and water his houseplants and stuff anyway."

"So just tell me, why don't you get a phone?" Bridget moved on to a second cornstalk. "I could understand your not wanting one while that slimy ex-husband was around. But now—"

"It's an expense." I couldn't really explain to anyone in affluent Palo Alto how I felt about expenses. My income was so marginal. The house payment Paul Drake made to me on his house was the first steady income I'd had in a long time. At the age of thirty-five, I felt the necessity of saving for the uncertain future—there was no pension fund in my life. I was currently without a writing assignment and losing a bit of sleep over that. I earned a little by teaching a writers' workshop at the senior center, and another dribble of income from selling the gourmet salad greens I grew in my yard to upscale restaurants in the area. That income would literally die when the first hard frost killed the lettuce and arugula in the raised beds I'd built at home. Then any sudden need for money would necessitate a jump into the temporary workers' pool, which is not a pleasant experience for me.

All in all, I made a point of not spending more than I had to. Perhaps it was an obsession. But I could do without a phone—it's intrusive, and it puts you at the beck and call of solicitors. While waiting for Drake to call the previous evening—all right, I had been sitting in his living room, reading his magazines, listening to his stereo, and waiting for him to call with an uneasy combination of anticipation and impatience—I had dealt with two rival telephone companies wanting to pitch their wares to Drake. That would drive me crazy if it were happening in my house. One of the solicitors asked me if I was Mrs. Paul Drake. All in all, it had been annoying.

"We haven't discussed Claudia's birthday yet." My feeble effort to change the subject failed.

"So what did Drake say when he called? Is his dad okay? Will he be back soon?"

"His dad is still in the ICU. Drake gave blood yesterday and they transfused his dad. As of last night, he was stabilized, but they want Drake to stick around in case they need more blood or bone marrow. He and his dad are compatible."

"That's not what I heard." Bridget shook her head. "I thought he never forgave them for naming him what they did."

"He's a grown-up. He's learned to live with that. Illness changes things." I thought about how Drake had looked when he'd gotten the call from his mother that his father, a retired Seattle policeman, had collapsed and been taken to the hospital. He'd been stunned by the possibility that his dad was at risk of dying. "He might be away through Thanksgiving if his dad doesn't respond to treatment quickly. His mom is devastated, evidently. He's gotten a leave from the police department until the first of December."

"That's hard." Bridget was quiet for a moment, hacking up another cornstalk. Moira grabbed more leaves and

24

tossed them up. The breeze obliged her, seizing the leaves and swirling them off.

"Hey!" Webster Powell stopped on the path, his hands on his hips. "Stop that! Those leaves are littering up my garden!"

Bridget and I exchanged exasperated glances, before she pasted on a smile and turned to Webster.

"Hi, Webster. Nothing could litter up your garden—it's impossibly neat. How do you do it?"

"I don't let little brats scatter mildew-laden junk all over everything." Webster was a tall, spare man, perhaps a couple of years younger than me. Even in garden clothes he was fastidious; the knees of his corduroy trousers were protected by pads, the gloves he slapped on one palm were immaculate, and his Dilbert T-shirt, proclaiming that technology was no place for wimps, was unstained by dirt. Only his boots, tall, green Wellingtons emblazoned with the Smith and Hawken logo, showed dark earth clinging to them.

His loud voice drew in Tamiko Frazier, who had the garden plot on the other side of his, across the path from mine. Her round face and graying hair, coupled with a vague look, were misleading; she knew more than anyone I'd ever met about garden lore. Her plot wasn't as tidy as Webster's, but it was fantastically productive. I owed her a lot; she often traded me her leftover fish meal or other soil amendments for the seedlings I had in abundance.

"Hello, Liz. Bridget." Tamiko nodded at us, then said, "Webster," her voice cooling. "This can't be that tiny baby, can it?" She smiled at Moira. "She's gotten so big."

Moira looked from her to Webster. Her little face was worried. She knew there was trouble.

"We aren't supposed to bring children who aren't old

25

enough to help," Webster said, moderating his voice. "And this isn't helpful!" He gestured to the yellowing shreds of corn leaves scattered over his perfectly mounded garden beds.

Tamiko narrowed her eyes. "Nonsense," she said, her soft voice turning steely. "It's all mulch, isn't it? And certainly better for the garden as a whole than Roundup, wouldn't you say?"

Webster stared at her, his mouth pressed tight, and then turned away. "I don't know what you're talking about." He strode up the path into his garden and unlocked his wheelbarrow, whirling the combination with quick, angry gestures. "But I won't tolerate people dumping their debris in my garden." Now he was glaring at me. "You put that Bermuda grass in my garden. I know you did. And if I ever catch you doing it again—"

Bridget looked at me, puzzled. "Liz doesn't have Bermuda grass in her garden. Why would she put it in yours?"

"I don't know." He pushed the wheelbarrow back to the main path. "But I'll find out. And when I do, you'll be out of the garden for good."

He marched away down the path, pushing the wheelbarrow in front of him.

# 4

**TAMIKO** looked after Webster as he trundled his wheelbarrow down the path. "Boy, he's got it in for you, doesn't he, Liz? I wonder why."

"I don't know." The sick feeling I'd been fighting all morning was back. "I didn't put any Bermuda grass in his garden. I have no idea why he thinks I did."

"Somebody's been rumormongering," Tamiko said. She was still staring after Webster. "This used to be such a nice group of people. Now everyone's always fighting. I don't understand what went wrong."

"Well, a good part of it is Lois." Bridget picked up Moira. "She's appointed herself garden cop, and the result is everyone's nitpicking everything to death. Before, we didn't mind a few weeds here and there. Now if everything's not perfect, she threatens to take your garden away."

"Let her try that on me." Tamiko straightened her dumpy form. She's a bit taller than I am, but then, I'm pretty short. "I believe in live-and-let-live, but I'm not going to keep my mouth shut if she's going around spreading rumors."

She marched back to her own plot. Bridget stared after her.

"Now, what was that all about? And why that crack about Roundup? Nobody here can use it, right? It's a pesticide, and we're organic."

"Nobody is supposed to, but rumor has it that Webster sprayed his Bermuda grass with it." I picked up the spade Bridget had discarded and began turning the cornstalks and beans into the ground. "I thought it was just a rumor, but his reaction makes me wonder."

"So that's how he gets rid of Bermuda grass." Bridget frowned. "And he has the gall to accuse me of wrongdoing."

"It's just a rumor." I regretted having repeated it. I know to my cost how often rumor and innuendo are wrong. "He's innocent until proven guilty."

"I'm going home, anyway." Bridget wore an unaccustomed expression of ire. "Nobody wants Moira here, and I've got a lot to do. If my garden isn't tidy enough, let Webster have it. I know that's what he wants."

"Could he have more than one? I didn't think that was allowed."

"Some people do. In fact, I heard that Lois has about six scattered around." Bridget dusted off Moira's dirty hands and looked around for her garden basket.

"Leave the shovel," I suggested. "I'll drop it off at your house later."

"Okay." Bridget picked up her basket, balancing Moira on one arm. "In fact, come by around two—I should be home for a while. And stay and have tea. We'll talk about Claudia's party then."

She left, using the south gate beside Tamiko's garden. I dug for a few more minutes, getting the cornstalks and beans well incorporated, and pulling up a bit more Bermuda grass. I pulled up the tomatoes, too, stacking

28

the cages neatly at the back of Bridget's garden, and cramming the withered vines into my bucket. Her garden plot looked much better when I finished. I picked up the bucket to carry over to the Dumpster, planning to fill it with wood chips on my way back and scatter them on her path. Then Lois wouldn't have any more reason to complain about Bridget.

Tamiko joined me as I went out the gate and turned right, walking on the perimeter path outside the garden fence. She glanced at my bucket of weeds and dead tomato vines. "You really made some progress today," she remarked. She, too, carried debris bundled in a tarp with handles. "These work days are a good idea for getting us moving with the fall cleanup."

"I still haven't gotten to my own plot, though." We rounded the corner and approached the area of fence that Lois was rebuilding to suit herself. She had gotten a couple of other people to put up the fence posts. They were pouring in concrete around the pressure-treated lumber as we went by. Lois gave me a baleful look, probably because I'd stopped doing her bidding.

"I saw Lois had you digging postholes." Tamiko glanced at me. "I didn't realize she was putting up a real fence there."

"Neither did Rita." I nodded at the garden manager, who stood by the Dumpster, making sure no one left their debris on the ground. She gave us her usual wide smile as we came up.

"The Dumpster is getting full," she announced.

"I'll pack it down, then." I swung myself up, not without effort, and stomped down on the tangle of weeds and other debris. Tamiko handed up her tarp and my bucket, and I stomped them in.

"Well, that was a good thought," Rita said. "I don't know if anyone else can get anything in there, though."

"What about this?" I turned around at the new voice. Carlotta Houseman stood beside the Dumpster, clutching a handful of Bermuda grass. I knew Carlotta from the senior writing workshop I led, although she was not a particularly welcome member.

"I can't reach, Liz." Her nasal whine grated on my ears just as it did in class. She smiled demurely. With her fluffy white hair and rounded body, she looked like everyone's dream grandmother. But I could see the malice in her expression.

Carlotta and I had tangled when I'd inherited my house from one of her neighbors. Carlotta had wanted me to join her in selling to a developer who planned to build townhouses. I had refused, and Carlotta had never forgiven me. Despite eventually realizing a tidy sum on her house, she still believed she could have gotten a better price if I had cooperated. And she seemed determined to make me sorry I hadn't followed her wishes.

"I didn't know you were a gardener, Carlotta."

"Oh, I'm just helping out a friend," Carlotta said sweetly. "Could you put this up there for me?" She batted her eyelashes helplessly at me.

"I guess." I took the Bermuda grass and chinned myself on the Dumpster again, getting it all in. Or so I thought.

"You dropped some," Carlotta observed, her faded eyes glinting. "But then, you're so careless with Bermuda grass. Aren't you, Liz?"

She turned and walked away, leaving me staring after her. Tamiko glanced from me to her.

"She's the one," she said under her breath.

"Excuse me?" Rita thrust herself between us. "What was that all about?"

"That woman, whoever she is, was going around this morning saying that Liz put Bermuda grass in Webster's garden, and maybe in a couple more. And some other nasty rumors, too." Tamiko regarded me thoughtfully. "Now, why would she want to do that? You know her, don't you, Liz?"

"I know her." I thought about the disruptions Carlotta had been causing in the writing workshop, the insinuations she kept making about my lack of morals and untrustworthiness. Evidently her whispering had fallen on fertile ground at the community garden. I watched her pause beside Lois and say something to her. They both turned to look at me. I regarded them steadily, and after a moment Lois looked away, her cheeks wearing bright spots of color. Carlotta continued to watch me, her small mouth pursed in a smile.

"Well, she's no friend of yours, believe me." Tamiko began to scoop some of the wood chips from a nearby pile onto her tarp. I helped her, wrinkling up my nose at the moldy dust that rose from the pile.

Rita tossed her ponytail. "Looks like Lois is making more trouble. I may have to do something about her."

"What could you do? She's got a lot of adherents in the garden." Tamiko asked the question as if it were all academic, and as far as I knew it was.

"I have some aces up my sleeve," Rita replied, looking smug. "And it's about time to play my cards. If you ladies will excuse me?"

She stalked purposefully toward Lois. I filled my bucket with wood chips and accompanied Tamiko back around the garden. Lois was in conversation with Rita when we passed, but we walked by quickly, motivated by a desire to put the whole thing behind us.

I finished tidying Bridget's garden and went over to my own. It looked pretty good; I grew things for my own table in it, since we weren't allowed to use anything we grew there for commercial purposes. It was handy to have a place for big stuff that took room—corn, pole beans, melons, squash. I filled a bucket with winter squash to take home, and defiantly left my own cornstalks up. I had already planted fava beans where the tomatoes and melons had been; those heavy feeders had left their beds depleted of nitrogen, and fava beans would help re-fix it. My path was free of weeds, my compost pile as tidy as it could be.

I felt very satisfied with it until I turned around and saw the small delegation blocking the end of my path. My good feelings shriveled up fast.

Lois stood with her mouth pinched up, staring at me. Beside her, Carlotta still wore the sly smile that denoted mischief-making. Webster lingered behind the two women, and several other gardeners whose names I didn't know crowded the path. All of them were looking at me with cold, accusing stares.

"So." Lois broke the silence. "Will you get a good price for those?" She pointed at the winter squash in my bucket.

"I don't sell the produce I grow here. You know that's not allowed." I tried to keep my voice even, not revealing that I felt trapped, put on trial.

"You were at the farmers' market last Saturday," Lois persisted. Carlotta crossed her arms over her chest, her smile broadening. I had seen her at the market the weekend before. Now I realized that this was a carefully orchestrated attack by her.

"I sold salad mix and winter greens from my home garden," I said. "Anyone who sells at the market has to have their home garden evaluated. Mine passed."

"You're growing salad mix here," Carlotta pointed out, unable to resist taunting me in person. "How do we know what you're selling didn't come from here?"

"Is this a trial?" I glanced around at the onlookers. A couple of them looked away. "If so, let's get all the facts out. Carlotta, why don't you tell all these people where you live?"

She stopped smiling. "What does that have to do with you breaking your agreement here?"

"Carlotta lives in Cupertino. You might ask her why she's using a garden designated for Palo Alto residents only."

"I'm not—" Carlotta began, then started over. "I'm just helping my friend." She glanced at Lois.

"And if you're not a gardener here, how would you know whether I spread Bermuda grass around other people's gardens or not?" A couple of the onlookers appeared struck by this. Webster's brows drew together. I saw that Tamiko had come over to stand by me, literally and, I hoped, figuratively.

"I didn't—"

"You did spread that rumor. I want to know why." I was angry, and I decided that my usual tactic of being meek and inoffensive and ducking trouble wouldn't get me anywhere. "You're doing the same thing at the senior center—another place you hang out that's for Palo Alto residents. If you have a problem with me, speak up. Don't make up these lies and expect to get away with it."

"It's slander, you know." Tamiko contributed this. "You could be sued." She glanced at me. "My daughter is an attorney. She could advise you about legal steps to take, Liz."

Carlotta's face mottled. "You can't prove anything," she hissed.

"She did say you threw the Bermuda grass on my garden." Webster looked confused. "Why would she say it if it wasn't true? And someone put it there."

"Why would you, Carlotta? Are you still blaming me for not selling my house when you sold yours? Do you still think you could have made more money if I'd done what you wanted?"

A couple of people moved away from Carlotta. Lois looked at her, too.

"You didn't tell me that when you talked about her," Lois said slowly. "You just said she was mixed up in that murder case last year. You made it sound like she'd gotten away with it."

Tamiko shook her head. "That is very serious. My daughter—"

"You're nuts, all of you." Carlotta's voice turned shrill. "I'm not the one who should be sued. She is!" She pointed at me. "She's breaking your rules. You should just kick her out!"

"That's not up to you, Carlotta. It's not even up to Lois or any of you." I looked at the hangers-on again. The ones who liked a scene were riveted, but several people had already drifted away. "If anyone is going to throw me out, it's Rita. And I think she has a better idea of what constitutes evidence than you do."

"Where is Rita?" Tamiko glanced around the garden. "She should be here to put a stop to this kind of thing. I don't like mean-spirited attacks in a place that should be devoted to peaceful horticulture."

"I'm going to go get her." Lois wheeled around. "We'll get to the bottom of this, I promise you."

"In the meantime," I said, picking up my bucket and pushing past Carlotta, "I'm putting my squash away. And I'm sure not inviting you over for a harvest dinner."

It was a mean crack, but I hadn't been so angry in a while. I try to avoid anger—it's a dangerous emotion that takes a person out of control, and control is very important to me.

I carried the bucket out to the parking lot and slid open the side door on my '69 VW microbus, nicknamed (because of its blue color and oxlike disposition) Babe. Barker greeted me enthusiastically. He'd been curled up on the backseat of the bus, which is the camper version (although without a pop-top).

Though I no longer had to live in Babe, both Barker and I regarded it as our traveling living room. When he saw I wasn't going to let him out, he hopped back up on the seat and assumed a long-suffering look. He took up a lot of room there.

I talked to him for a few minutes, and made sure his water dish was accessible. The sun had warmed the inside of the bus since I'd parked, so I cranked the side windows wider and opened the roof vent.

Leaving Barker with the squash, I went back to the garden for my tools. Tamiko was no longer working in her plot beside the gate; Webster, too, was not in sight. A low murmur swept through the garden on the wind, coming from the side near Lois's plot. I could see a group of people congregated there. For a minute I hesitated, not willing to run the gauntlet of yet more suspicion and

35

malice. Finally I walked along the path past other plots, some well-tended and some overgrown, past the tall stalks and empty heads of sunflowers, the various composting methods people had devised, the thick hedges of raspberries and the twining stems of grapevines.

The path grew crowded, blocked by people, who glanced at me and moved away until I could see into the center of it. The noise of busy whispering filled the air like a swarm of bees.

Straight ahead, Lois knelt in the dirt of her garden plot beside a trench she'd been working on as part of a course of double-digging, her hands pressed to her chest. The trench so carefully emptied of dirt was instead full of a tumble of pale flesh and spandex and brassy blond hair.

Rita. It took only a cursory look to see that, with her head twisted so uncomfortably away from her body, she couldn't still be alive. Even though her bright blue eyes were open, staring sightlessly at the sky.

# 5

AT least no one was looking at me, for the simple reason that they couldn't take their eyes off Rita's body. I could feel the speculation, the sense of being branded. It would seem very pat to the gardeners. Carlotta whispers it around that I have gotten away with murder, and—presto—a suspicious death crops up.

Carlotta herself stood at one side, her expression an interesting mix of horror and avid speculation. When she saw me watching her, that malicious smile appeared. Perhaps it was one of these nervous reactions people get in moments of stress. Whatever, it drove me far enough out of my self-control to speak.

"There's nothing funny about this, Carlotta."

Her head and shoulders pulled back, her eyes widened in surprise. "I don't know what you're talking about," she said, her voice huffy.

A couple of people stepped farther away, as if to leave us in the ring together.

Our voices seemed to bring Lois out of a trance. She began tugging at Rita's foot. "Get her out of here," she cried, her voice growing shrill. "Get her out of my plot!"

I reached along the well-mulched path, grabbing for Lois's arm. "You shouldn't touch the body." I looked around at the circle of shocked faces. "She is dead, I presume? Did someone check?"

A tall black man, holding himself a little aloof, raised his hand. "I'm a doctor. I heard the commotion and came over, thinking there was an accident. I couldn't find a pulse, so I left the area untouched."

"I've called 911," a woman at one side of the crowd volunteered. She held her cell phone to her ear. "The police and paramedics are on their way."

"Lois is going to be in trouble if she doesn't get out of there." I didn't care if Lois got in trouble or not, but I felt compassion for Bruno Morales, Drake's partner in homicide investigations. Palo Alto has few homicides, so the two of them mostly work on other cases. This would turn up on Bruno's plate, and with Drake out of town, he would be swamped.

"She's not the only one," Carlotta muttered, loud enough for everyone to hear.

That did it. "As Lois has informed all of you," I said, "I have been involved in a murder investigation." A few people gasped. Carlotta narrowed her eyes, sensing that I would steal her thunder. "I wasn't convicted or even charged with that crime. In fact, Carlotta herself was a suspect in it. Due to that experience, we both know to tell you to keep clear of the area around the victim. Stay in the garden; if the police find out you were here and left before they arrived, they'll draw their own conclusions. And tell them everything you know or saw. Their job is sorting through stuff till they get to the truth. If you don't tell them everything, you could make it difficult for both you and them later."

The circle of gardeners backed obediently away from Lois's plot. Most of them stayed on the paths, too, although the fava beans in a nearby plot had been severely trampled. The doctor went to Lois, helping her up and leading her away.

"It's sacrilege, that's what," Lois sniffled. The doctor patted her arm, making soothing sounds. "My poor Sidney! Whatever would he think? They have to get her out of there. She's ruining everything!"

I found that little snippet of conversation puzzling. But the police and paramedics arrived just then, heralded by sirens, and we all had enough to look at while they conferred over Rita's body, secured the scene, and talked to gardeners.

I recognized Rhea, one of the officers writing down names and addresses. She recognized me, too.

"Liz. I didn't know you were a community gardener." She glanced over her shoulder at the forensics team, who had put up a perimeter around Lois's garden, taking in big chunks of neighboring gardens and paths. The gardeners wouldn't like that, but death has many unpleasant consequences.

"Yeah, I've been gardening here for about four years now."

Rhea regarded me thoughtfully. "So you know a lot of background. Bruno will want to talk to you." She grinned. "He's going to be upset at having to share this one with the county, since Drake is gone."

"So he won't be able to do the investigation alone?"

She shrugged. "Maybe. Us uniforms are not always on top of how assignments are made." She looked at the doctor and Lois, who had been joined by one of the paramedics. "That the guy who made the corpse?"

"He said he felt for a pulse, didn't find one, backed

off." I nodded toward Lois. "She has that plot. It's really upset her, obviously."

Rhea shook her head. "Not a nice thing to find." Her gaze drifted back to Rita's body. Bruno Morales came around the corner of the equipment shed that concealed the library parking lots from the garden, and Rhea's attention sharpened. "I'm going to check in with the man. Stick around, now."

She gave me a friendly smile as she turned to leave.

"Oh, Rhea—" I caught her arm.

"Yeah?" She shut her notebook, looking inquiringly at me.

"There's a woman over there." I flicked my gaze toward Carlotta, who was watching my encounter with the police intently. "She was one of the neighbors in that case last fall, and she's told all the gardeners I was a murder suspect and that there's something shady about me. I'm sure you'll hear about that as you take statements."

"Bit of a bigmouth, isn't she?" Rhea regarded Carlotta with disfavor. "I'll certainly want to take her statement. I'll make sure she doesn't leave."

She walked over to Carlotta and said something that made the older woman sputter, then went on to Lois's plot, where Bruno was in consultation with the forensics team. Seeing Carlotta heading for me, I followed Rhea, trying to stay discreetly in the background, but close enough to the police that I could avoid Carlotta.

Bruno squatted beside the garden plot, studying the scene. I tried not to look at Rita's livid face, tried not to notice the dead shine of her brassy hair.

I couldn't hear what Bruno said, but periodically he picked up bits of stuff and handed them over his shoulder, where one of the forensics team jarred or bagged it and wrote all over the container.

Inching closer, I heard the man with the jars address Bruno.

"So whaddaya think, Morales? Accident?"

I felt like an idiot. It hadn't even occurred to me that it could be an accident. In my recent experience, unexpected death wasn't.

I looked closer at the scene. Rita's body lay half in, half out of a foot-and-a-half-deep trench dug across the ten-foot width of the bed. In the French Intensive manner, the surface of the bed rose in a low mound above ground level. Obviously Lois had dug her bed within the last couple of seasons, and shouldn't have had to do it again. This style of gardening is characterized by keeping the earth aerated, never standing directly on the dirt, loosening the soil to a depth of eighteen inches after first removing the top layer to avoid mixing it in with subsoil. Although the ground in Palo Alto is adobe clay, which most gardeners find undesirable, I think it's great. When dug while moist, it's rich and dark as far down as you go. Adding soil amendments makes it friable, and it holds moisture much better than the sandy soils closer to the coast.

One of the uniforms pointed to the rake that lay at an angle on the ground, half in the path, half on the bed. "Maybe she stumbled across that and fell backwards, hitting her neck on the edge of that hole." He shook his head. "Crazy way to garden, digging big holes."

"You fill each trench in when you dig the next trench." Bruno sounded absentminded. I wasn't too surprised that he knew the principles of double-digging. He knew a lot about a number of things. "You see how loose the soil is

41

at this end, where the gardener has already filled the trenches?" He pushed his fingers into the soil appreciatively, then carefully patted it back down. "The soft dirt takes good impressions."

"But there aren't any impressions," the uniform argued.

"My point exactly." Bruno looked up at him. "She couldn't have been in the plot, or we would see the impressions of her shoes." He nodded at the soles of Rita's high-top aerobic shoes. "And we would see loose dirt on her soles." He moved around the plot to put plastic bags over Rita's shoes, taking them off her feet with all traces and clues safely bagged. I wondered if he knew that Lois had been shaking one of those feet, maybe shaking clues right off it.

"Maybe the rake was in the path." The uniform wouldn't give up.

Bruno got his head right down on the ground, looking across the surface of the path. "She stood here." He touched the fresh bark that covered the path. "This does not take good footprints. But from her position, she was facing away from the trench. She fell backward; might have hit her head on the edge of the trench and so broken her neck. But what made her fall?"

"Or was she pushed?" The uniform shrugged. "Hard to say at this point."

"I think we will find something in the postmortem." Bruno stood up. "Have the pictures been taken? Good. You can remove her now." He stood beside the trench, his face sober, while the paramedics bundled up Rita and wheeled her away.

Turning, he saw me. "Liz. Of course, you have a garden here. Do you know anything about this?"

42

"I don't know what happened, but there has been some tension this morning."

"Of course." Bruno sighed. "Why don't you come over here and tell me about it? Then I can let you leave."

"Maybe you won't want to, after you hear what I say."

He stopped in the middle of pulling his laptop out of its case and looked at me sharply. "What are you saying, Liz? You pushed that woman into the trench?"

"No. Nothing like that." I waited until he got the laptop steady on the nearest fence post, his fingers poised expectantly on the keys, and then I started talking about the visit from Lois the day before, with its vaguely threatening tone. "She said if I didn't come to the work day, I'd be sorry. I would have thought it was a joke, but she didn't laugh."

He stopped typing for a moment and looked at me seriously. "So you came?"

"Yes. She gave me a really hard task—to dig all these postholes. And she was—triumphant, as if she had me in her power somehow." I glanced across the garden. Lois and Carlotta stood together. They were talking, both frowning. I wondered at their alliance.

Bruno wrote down the rest of the story—Carlotta's strange harassment, the revelation of my previous suspect-hood. There were certainly worse things about my life Carlotta could have chosen to reveal. I thanked my lucky stars she wasn't much of a researcher. I wouldn't have wanted my relationship with my ex-husband spread all over town, or the stint I served in prison for trying to kill him before he killed me. He had lived through that, and for a number of years thereafter, and I wasn't sorry that someone else had finally induced him to leave this world.

But his death, added to those other bodies that kept tumbling into my life, might have made even a well-wisher stop to think. Certainly they had made me wonder.

Bruno looked at me, his hands on the keyboard. I hurried to finish my story. "Then I went out to my bus to put away my veggies, and when I came back everyone was over at Lois's plot, looking at the body." I shivered. "Do you think it might have been an accident?"

Bruno typed a little more before he answered. "At this point I do not think. I merely record." He closed the laptop. His brown eyes were liquid with sympathy. "I am sorry, Liz."

I felt even colder. "Sorry for what?"

"For the pain this woman brings you by dragging up that past history."

I studied him, and he looked away. "There's more to it than that, isn't there? You will have to bring up the past history as well. In other words, I'm a suspect again."

"I would not say that," Bruno broke in. "You will be involved in our investigation." He looked around at the steady stream of gardeners, leaving after having given their names and addresses to the police. "Many people will be involved." His eyes sharpened on Carlotta, who stood with a few others, watching as the evidence specialists sifted through the dirt. Lois was at the gate, waving her petition at the departing gardeners. Bruno sighed. "It will not be easy, evidently." His gaze came back to mine. "Be very careful, Liz. You seem to have at least one enemy."

A few hours earlier, I would have laughed about Carlotta as any kind of effective enemy. But now I had to wonder. How far would she go to get me into trouble?

# 6

**BRIDGET** reached across the table and angled the chipped spout of her big teapot, pouring a stream of fragrant jasmine tea into my cup. "Incredible," she said finally.

"Yeah. Count yourself lucky you left when you did."

She shivered. "I wish I'd stayed to help you out. If I'd been with you, there'd have been no question—"

"I'm not really under suspicion, any more than anyone else there. I bet most of the gardeners were in my position—working alone, no one able to vouch for them every minute. In fact, Rita's death probably was an accident."

Bridget shook her head. "I don't know. The tension there was pretty thick this morning. With Rita and Lois both throwing their weight around—"

"Surely you don't think Lois would do this?" Usually, Bridget is the person who defends everyone's right to be considered innocent until proven guilty.

"I think Lois might be capable of shoving Rita if she lost her temper." Bridget spoke after taking a moment to think. "But I would be surprised if Rita didn't push her back, and frankly, I would expect Rita to do more damage. She's—she was—a hefty woman."

"So you think it was an accident, and the person responsible got cold feet and hasn't come forward."

"Yes, and that doesn't exactly sound like Lois. She would be screaming away about it, blaming Rita for everything."

"Maybe." It was my turn to shiver. "She might have been too shocked to speak or make sense. Committing a violent act can be so surprising."

"Stop kicking yourself about something that happened years ago." Bridget's voice was stern, but she patted my hand. "What you did wasn't violence so much as self-defense. There's a difference between trying to save your life and overindulging in a temper tantrum. When are you going to let that old history go?"

She pushed the plate of cookies closer, as if they could, lotus-like, aid me in forgetting that I had once aimed a gun, pulled the trigger, sent a bullet burrowing through flesh, blood vessels, bone. The act had probably saved my life; my husband had been stopped before he could finish teaching me whatever lesson it was I couldn't seem to learn. He didn't die—then, at least. I went to jail, where I was, paradoxically, free of him. I got a divorce without the usual peril attending separation from a batterer; Tony couldn't get at me to make me permanently sorry. And then after my parole, I eluded him for years, while I tried to make his looming threat fill less of my psyche.

No matter how far I came in this exercise, he still took up a dark corner in my head, small but potent, like a black hole waiting to suck everything into itself. His eventual death at someone else's hands had only decreased the darkness, not removed it entirely.

I took one of the cookies, and Bridget smiled in relief.

The counter behind us was covered with cookies, their sweet aroma filling the air. The Montrose house was relatively quiet, unusual for a Saturday afternoon. The big round table in the kitchen's bay window had been recently tidied and set with clean place mats and the tea things. In the living room, Moira hummed to herself while involved in her latest accomplishment, fitting fat plastic blocks together to build a lopsided tower. An absence of blasting noises and shrieks indicated that the three Montrose boys were elsewhere.

"These are great." I took a second cookie, not to make Bridget feel better, but on my own account.

"Preschool work day." Bridget glanced at the clock. "Emery took the boys over, but I'm not going for another hour. So we have some time to put our heads together and figure out who would want Rita dead."

"The police are already doing that, and with far more likelihood of success than we'll have." I resisted the urge for another cookie. "I don't know anything about Rita other than her work as the garden coordinator."

"Me neither." Bridget looked smug. "But I know who might know something about her. And she'll be here any minute."

"Melanie." I sat back in the chair, sipping my cooling tea.

"She's coming over to plan the birthday party."

"Which we haven't begun to plan."

Bridget waved that away. "We'll get to it. Murder is more important."

"We don't know it's murder."

Bridget sobered. "True. But I'm afraid it is. And that puts you in danger, Liz. Someone may think you make a convenient scapegoat. It's happened before."

"You don't know how special that makes me feel." I

set down the cup a little harder than I meant to. "What is it about me? I just want to keep a low profile and tend my gardens."

The doorbell rang. Bridget went to answer it. From my chair, I could see through the kitchen doorway into the living room. Melanie Dixon, her streaked brown hair perfectly arranged, led her equally cute little daughter into the house. Susanna dashed across the living room to join Moira, waving her flaxen-haired doll, which promptly nose-dived into Moira's tower. Susanna screamed with laughter. Moira burst into tears.

"I don't know what makes Susanna so boisterous here," Melanie said, frowning at Susanna while Bridget comforted Moira. Susanna, too, patted her back, murmuring, "It's okay, baby. Don't cry, baby." She sat on the floor and took more blocks out of the bin. "I build a big tower. Then she can crash."

After a few minutes, the moms joined me at the table. Melanie gave me a brief smile. "Hello, Liz."

"Melanie."

She accepted the cup of tea Bridget poured, but refused a cookie. I squelched the surge of irritation Melanie always inspired in me. She and Bridget had worked together before having children, and they also belonged to the local poets' group. I knew they had things in common, but they were polar opposites as far as I was concerned.

"When exactly is Claudia's birthday? This is a very busy time for me." Melanie pulled a leather-bound calendar from her Gucci bag. I wouldn't have known it was Gucci if my niece, Amy, hadn't educated me on one of our swings through the secondhand stores. "Let's see." Melanie opened the calendar. "Is it before Thanksgiving?"

"It's next Wednesday." Bridget took a cookie for herself. "I'll just have one, and really savor it," she told Melanie, who had glanced pointedly at Bridget's comfortably rounded figure.

"On your hips be it." Melanie sipped her tea, but couldn't resist glancing at the cookie plate. "Oh, well, if everyone else is going to eat them—" She reached out and broke off a piece. "Next Wednesday? That appears to be free." She sounded puzzled, as if unable to believe she had a free day.

"And you're available, right, Liz?"

"If I'm not arrested." It slipped out before I remembered that Melanie had no sense of humor.

"Arrested? What have you done now?" Surreptitiously she broke off another piece of cookie.

Bridget shushed me with a glance. "Do you know the Danceys? The family with the big construction business?"

"The boys were at Paly when I was," Melanie said guardedly, using the local name for Palo Alto High School. "I don't really know them that well. They've done some work for us."

"Who exactly runs that construction company?"

"Jack Dancey, the old man, stepped down a couple of years ago," Melanie said thoughtfully. "I had Dwight over to bid on the bathroom remodel we did, and he told me that he and Tom were running the company, that his dad had pretty much retired. And then he fobbed the job off on his foreman, who didn't even speak English." Melanie's lips tightened. "I soon let him know that wasn't acceptable."

"Are those the only ones, Tom and Dwight? I thought there was a girl."

Melanie pursed her lips. "Well, Jack remarried when

the boys were in high school. His new wife had a younger daughter, I think."

"That's Rita, the community garden coordinator."

Melanie searched her memory. "That's right. She must have been ten at least when her mom married. She uses the name Dancey, though I don't think Jack adopted her. Now I remember meeting her at one of the city functions. Tom came with her, and everyone was whispering that Dancey's had a big housing project up for approval and he was hoping to expedite the process. And I think there was a little juicy gossip about Tom and Rita having a fling, even though they were stepbrother and -sister."

"Is that so?" Bridget was listening intently. I didn't see what this had to do with the garden. But maybe whoever had killed Rita had come from a different area of her life. "And did Tom Dancey get preferential treatment for his project?"

"Not likely." Melanie gave in and took the rest of the cookie. "You know how the city bends over backwards to avoid looking like they play favorites. And expedite isn't in the game plan in this town. I don't think that housing has been built yet. Still hung up in the permit process."

"So Rita might have been using her position to give her stepbrother a competitive edge in finding out about city projects." Bridget looked at me.

"Yeah." It sounded like something Rita would do. "And she did say something about her stepfather being in construction, when she was arguing with Lois about the fence."

Melanie pouted. "So what is going on here? Why do we care about the Danceys? What has this got to do with Claudia's birthday?"

"Rita was killed today at the garden."

Melanie gaped.

"We don't know that she was killed, for sure," I hastened to add to Bridget's stark announcement. "But she's dead, all right."

"That's terrible." Melanie leaned forward, her nose for news twitching. "What happened?"

"We don't know," I said. "She was found dead in a garden plot. Her neck was broken. She might have tripped on a rake and fallen into the trench the gardener had been digging."

"Goodness." Melanie took a moment to absorb it. "The police are staying busy these days."

The front door burst open and Emery Montrose charged in, towing the youngest boy, Mick. "Gotta find a hammer," he gasped, collapsing at the table. Mick, released, grabbed a cookie and went to see what the girls were doing. Emery wiped his arm across his face.

"Is it an emergency?" Bridget was on her feet.

"No. But there's only one hammer and it's always in demand, so I said I'd get another one. And Mick was bored anyway. He doesn't want to do the work day anymore."

"What about Corky and Sam?"

"They're fine." Emery accepted the glass of sparkling water she poured for him. "It's far more effort to jog with a three-year-old than to jog alone. Mick's gotten a lot heavier, hasn't he?"

"Anything you carry when you run will get heavy." Bridget spoke from experience. She jogs, too, when she can get free of her children. Her focus is on time, not distance—she runs for ten minutes, turns around, runs back. I've done it with her—it's not too taxing to go at her speed. But it wouldn't be fun carrying a squirmy three-year-old at the same time.

"Guess I'd better take the hammer and get back." Emery drained his glass, seized two cookies, and stood up. "Nice sitting with you ladies, if only for a moment." He looked at Bridget. "I'm leaving Mick here, okay?"

"Fine." Bridget looked into the living room. Mick and Susanna had commandeered the plastic blocks. Moira was busy sticking bristle blocks into Susanna's doll's long blond hair.

Emery vanished out the back door, toward the garage and his workshop. Melanie pushed back her chair.

"If we're through planning Claudia's birthday party—"

"We haven't even started." Bridget barred the kitchen door. "And, Melanie, this stuff about Rita is confidential. No gossiping."

"I don't gossip." Melanie drew herself up. "I was merely planning to mention it to a few people who might know more about the Danceys than I do." She put her calendar back in her bag. "And what's left to plan? Claudia's party, Wednesday night."

"We'll have it here." Bridget scrawled something on her own calendar, a huge one that hung on the back of the swinging kitchen door. "I'll ask Claudia to dinner. No, I'll ask her to baby-sit while Emery and I go out to dinner. Then she won't suspect anything."

"Do you think a surprise party is wise? Some people really hate to be surprised." Melanie offered this bit of wisdom just before breaking off another piece of cookie.

"She'll love it." Bridget put down the pencil. "I'll make lasagna and garlic bread."

"I'll order a cake." Melanie whipped out her planner again. "Gotta run, Bridget. Nice seeing you, Liz."

"I'll do the salad." I wanted to do something for Claudia, too. I hated it when everyone acted as if I were too poor to contribute.

"Great," Bridget said briskly. "Bring a lot. I'm going to let some of the other poets know. They can bring wine."

The planning was over. Melanie spent a couple of minutes picking the bristle blocks out of the doll's hair while Moira used her own battered doll to destroy the fort Mick and Susanna had built.

"Liz," Bridget said, after Melanie had left, catching me at the door. "Come over tonight for dinner. We're not doing anything."

"I've got to be back at Drake's by eight."

"We'll be done by then. Come at six."

I knew Bridget was indulging in an excess of mothering, but it had its desired effect. I felt comforted, not alone anymore, even though there was no one but Barker waiting for me when I got back to my house.

# 7

**BARKER** sniffed around the yard, refreshing his territorial markings everywhere. My yard is pretty good-sized by Palo Alto standards. The two houses I'd inherited, much to Carlotta's disgust, had been on an extra-long lot. Drake's house had a small front yard that faced the street and a gravel area for parking directly behind his back door. The rest was mine.

It felt funny to be missing Drake. At the time he'd bought the house from me, he'd been no more than the police detective who'd had charge of investigating a murder I'd been suspected of committing.

Now I kept thinking about him while I cleaned my gardening tools and put them away in the garage. I wanted him to call that evening, wanted to know about his father's illness, how he and his mother were holding up.

But I dreaded his call, too. He had his laptop with him, and I knew he got e-mail from Bruno Morales. He'd probably ask me about Rita's death. Being out of the investigative loop would make him crazy. And he'd give me a lot of grief for getting mixed up in it. As if there were any way I could have avoided it.

My little cottage may be rickety, but at least I own it

free and clear. I fix it up as I have time and money, which is to say, I don't fix it much. The foundation has settled around the front porch, leaving the steps gently canted to one side. I hoped the porch wouldn't fall off before I got enough money ahead to take care of the problem.

I weeded through the flower bed that edged the picket fence separating my front lawn from Drake's parking area. The roses planted there were attention hogs, always wanting their diseased leaves stripped off and yummy amendments fed to them. I was letting hips form for the winter, but there were still a few buds and blossoms. I raked up the yellow leaves that had fallen to the ground, and attacked some renegade violets. Whoever said violets were shy, shrinking flowers was wrong. They're aggressive invaders, capable of beating back ivy in a single season. I thought they were pretty when they popped up along the edge of my flower bed, but their relentless advance was changing my mind.

I was still on my knees in front of the roses when Barker growled. Peering through the foliage toward the street, I saw Lois heading down the driveway again, like some horrid déjà vu. She had nearly reached the fence when Barker went into his ravening-dog routine.

"Nice doggie," she quavered. She hadn't yet seen me. I thought of crouching behind the fence until she went away.

Barker ran along the gate, growling maniacally. I hoped he remembered that he wasn't allowed to leap over it. When I'd put it up, while he was a puppy, I'd had no clue that he would one day be so large, with such long legs.

Lois wouldn't have been enough to tempt him to jump, if she hadn't gotten frightened and begun backing stealthily away, in a manner very enticing to a young and enthusiastic dog.

Reluctantly I got to my feet. "Back," I said in my sternest voice. "To the porch, Barker."

He complied, though glancing at me a couple of times to make sure I really meant it. When he sat on the porch, I turned to Lois.

"Will he bite?" She was frozen to the driveway, her gaze fixed on Barker as if he were the Antichrist.

"Maybe. He is protective of his space." I doubted that he would bite; he's more interested in playing. But I wasn't about to reveal his pussycat nature to someone who might not have my best interests at heart. "Why are you here, Lois?"

She came a step nearer. "As long as questions have been raised, I have a duty to investigate."

"Questions?"

"About you selling the things you grow in the community garden. That's absolutely forbidden." Since Barker stayed on the porch, she came right up to the gate. "I want to check out your claim that you only sell what you grow here." She looked around, taking in the raised beds that marched along the back of the yard. "You have a fair amount of space, I'll say that. I didn't notice yesterday." She sounded disappointed.

"Check me out, by all means." I opened the gate, and Barker leapt to his feet.

Lois hesitated. "Can't you put the dog inside?"

"No." I was angry all over again. And in the face of her rudeness, there didn't seem to be much reason for polite pretense. "Just don't yell at me and he won't attack you."

I shut the gate behind Lois. Once she was in, she

seemed reluctant to start her inspection. "Oh, what lovely roses. Do you sell flowers, too?"

"No. I like to have flowers to give to my friends." I had been thinking while I weeded that the buds on Margaret Merrill and Oklahoma would make a nice centerpiece for Claudia's birthday party. She, too, was fond of roses.

"The veggies are over here," I said, and led the way to the raised beds.

Barker followed us, his nose extremely interested in Lois's pant legs. She winced away, but he couldn't be discouraged. "You must have cats," I said, finally snapping my fingers to make him leave her alone. "He loves cats."

Lois shivered. "I can imagine."

We stopped beside the beds of salad mix and root vegetables. A few cherry tomato plants still produced in one bed, next to the brilliant ruby ribs of kale.

Lois inspected, her knife-blade nose twitching. "What's this?" She was looking at one bed full of stubby, chopped-off plants.

"That's where I harvested salad mix for the farmers' market last week. It takes a couple of weeks to come back, so I have several beds in rotation." I showed her the setup. "I cut this one the week before, and this one a month ago. You see it's ready to cut again."

"That's not a very big crop." She looked at the bed, full of bronze and green foliage, with feathery, pastel frisée and dark red radicchio providing highlights, and sniffed disdainfully.

"Right." I wanted her out of my yard. From her point of view, the raised beds I had built with lumber scavenged from construction sites were slipshod and mismatched. My house was shabby, not comfortably worn.

My cold frames were patched together, not an ingenious use of old storm windows.

"Carlotta said you were probably growing something illegal here as well." Lois peered into the backyard as if I might have a nice raised bed full of marijuana plants. "She said, how can you live in a place like Palo Alto if this is all the money you earn?"

I took her arm, not gently, and marched her toward the gate. "You and Carlotta can jump in the lake. You've seen what you came for. Now get out."

She pulled her arm free and faced me. "I'm not done yet," she protested. "What's got you so mad, anyway?"

"Lois, you come here, you insult me, you imply I'm a criminal—"

"Aren't you?" Her face showed genuine puzzlement. "Carlotta said—"

"I don't give a rat's ass what Carlotta said." Barker came and stood beside me, his hackles raised. Lois glanced at him, uncomfortable. "She knows nothing about me. Her tiny brain has only one thought in it—that I should have done what she wanted. Maybe she never learned that people don't have to do what she wants. Of course, with you licking her lying boots, it seems she doesn't have to learn."

Lois gasped. I felt ashamed of myself briefly, as if my mother's astral body stood at my elbow and pinched my arm with disapproval.

"I wanted to say," Lois began after a moment, "that I didn't believe what Carlotta said about you shooting your ex-husband."

"Well, believe it."

"And you went to jail and everything?" Lois was avid for details. "I can't believe it. You seem so quiet."

58

"I'll try to be noisier." I stepped forward to usher her through the gate. She didn't move.

"Nevertheless, Carlotta shouldn't say you killed Rita to keep her from telling that you sell what you grow in the community garden. I came to see for myself, and I see she's wrong." She spoke with a huffy dignity.

"Oh." Some of my anger drained away. "Well, thanks, I guess."

"You're welcome." Lois inclined her head graciously. "It didn't make any sense for her to say that. You weren't the one who thought Rita—" She stopped.

"Thought Rita what?"

Lois veered away from that topic. "I have been—very upset," she announced, and I could see by the watery shine of her faded eyes that she was close to tears. "My sainted Sidney! It was more than I could take. And then Carlotta said—" She took a hankie out of the large, tan handbag that hung from her bony arm, and burst into sobs.

I began to think I'd have her on my hands for the rest of the afternoon. "Maybe," I said in desperation, "you should come in and have a glass of water or something. Did you eat any lunch?"

She let me guide her up onto the porch and into the living room. "I don't remember," she sniffed finally. "It's all been just horrible. Horrible." She wiped her eyes and put away the handkerchief, resting her skinny hand on my arm. "If I said something that offended you, I'm sorry. I'm just not myself right now."

I thought she'd seemed very much like herself. It was this nicer Lois I didn't recognize. "I'll get you a drink."

She followed me into the kitchen, gazing around in frank curiosity. There's not much to see—old linoleum on the floor, old white-painted wood cabinets around the walls. "That's Vivien's kitchen table, isn't it?" She pointed at the dinette set with its red Formica top. I polished it every so often, and the chrome legs gleamed. I'd even been able to repair the rips in the vinyl chair seats. "You've kept it very nice."

"I think of Vivien every day." This was true. I just hadn't meant to let it slip out to an unsympathetic person like Lois. She nodded her head in agreement, though.

"She was a lovely person. We were in the same bridge club for a couple of years. I always thought Carlotta was off-base to pressure her to sell her home. And she was well within her rights to leave it to you, I suppose." Big of her to concede that. "Certainly it's better to have people living in houses than parking around in their cars." The disapproval was back in her voice. She accepted the glass of water I gave her and sipped it slowly, checking out the curtains I'd made from a cheerful red and yellow thrift-store tablecloth.

"So, about Rita—" I began.

"You have a lot of papers in there." Carlotta looked through the kitchen door. Manuscripts in various stages of completion were piled around my elderly computer. "Are you a typist or something?"

"I'm a writer, as Carlotta no doubt told you." Carlotta was not currently enrolled in the writing workshop I taught for the senior center downtown, but that didn't stop her from coming by to harass me. Anyone who sold to such a motley collection of magazines, she'd tell my students after the class, couldn't be much of a writer. It's true that *Organic Gardening* and *True Confessions*—both of which had bought pieces from me, though not on the same subject—don't pay well. But I had sold an article to *Smithsonian*, and that, I felt, boosted my stock considerably.

"Where do you get your ideas?" Lois sipped daintily at her water. She eyed one of the red vinyl seats, as if planning to settle in for a cozy afternoon's gossip. In light of Rita's death, it was too surreal.

"Lois, what did you mean about Rita? You started to say that someone was angry at her, didn't you?"

Lois set the water down on the table. "For your information, I know nothing about Rita's death. All I know is, however she died, she's desecrated my beloved Sidney. I should have known a low-class girl like that was trouble from the get-go."

"Sidney?" I interrupted what promised to be the usual tirade on Rita's bad behavior. "What does Sidney have to do with this?"

"He can't do anything. He's been dead for over a year." Lois was indignant. "And I'll thank you not to mention him so disrespectfully. You barely knew him. He's Mr. Humphries to you."

"Mr. Humphries, as you point out, is dead. So how does Rita's death relate to his?" I started to have wild ideas about Lois as some kind of twisted, elderly serial killer.

"So you hadn't guessed. I thought you had. Rita did." Her lips pinched together.

"Guessed about—"

"About Sidney. Being there." She leaned closer and lowered her voice. "In the shrine. You know—that little wooden chest. You called it a shrine one day. That's why I thought you knew. I've been so worried that you would tell. Rita said—" She bit her lip.

It was all starting to come clear. "You have your husband buried in your community garden plot?"

"Just his ashes," she said quickly. "He wanted it, you know. He spent hours every day at our garden." Her eyes shone with tears again. "It was the happiest time of our lives. He built the little shrine before he died and made me promise, and of course I've kept my promise." She drew herself up, putting the hankie away again. "No matter what Rita said, Sidney stays, and that's that. And whoever profaned his resting place by killing her there is going to pay."

I watched, dumbfounded, as Lois stalked from the room. I was just in time to catch the front door after she flung it open.

"Lois, wait—"

"I'm busy," she snapped over her shoulder. "Some of us want to know what really happened, you know."

She crunched her way down the drive. Barker and I looked at each other, and then I went out to finish my weeding.

# 8

**IT** was nearly dinnertime when I finished weeding. I let Barker into the house and was following him when I heard, faintly, Drake's ringing telephone. I hadn't expected to hear from him until later that evening, but I didn't want to miss his call if he was early.

Keys in hand, I raced for his back door, and picked up the phone just before the answering machine did.

"Did you, like, run all the way from your house?" My seventeen-year-old niece, Amy, answered my breathless greeting. "This is so cool, because I didn't think I'd actually, like, be talking to you, since you don't even live there. I was just going to leave a message. You should get your own phone, Aunt Liz."

I said, through gritted teeth, "Hi, Amy. I ran for the phone because I'm expecting a call."

"Oh. Well—"

"But it's nice talking to you." I tried to sound more enthusiastic. "What's happening?"

Amy hesitated. "See, there's this amazing thing. Our school burned down."

"What?" I pictured the high school, the same one I had attended in Denver in my own far-off youth. The last time I'd been back, it hadn't looked the same, though—it had sprawled into a huge complex of more than a dozen buildings. "All of that's gone?"

"Not gone exactly." I could almost see Amy's shrug, her wide grin. "I mean, the fire started in the cafeteria, and it's, like, gutted, along with the gym. Everything else is just smoke-damaged and all wet and stinky and stuff. So we get off until after Thanksgiving, while they clean it up."

"Great. Sounds like you'll get a long vacation." I glanced at the calendar that hangs above Drake's phone. Counting the Thanksgiving holiday, she had nearly two weeks off. "It'll be a drag making all that up."

"Yeah, we have to go to school right up to Christmas. The skiers and shredders are totally bummed. But I don't care."

"Shredders?"

"You know—the snowboarders." Amy sounded impatient, but she didn't go on with her story. It wasn't like her.

"Drake's in Seattle right now," I said, rushing to fill that unnerving silence. "His dad's real sick. He's supposed to call about it, and I should really keep the line free—"

Amy interrupted, her voice urgent. "I thought it would be a good idea for me to come out and visit you—make, like, a college visit, see? Juniors on college track are supposed to visit schools we want to go to, and I definitely want to go out there."

"I just saw in the paper that most everyone in Stanford's freshman class is a valedictorian."

"My grades are okay." Amy shrugged away this reality check. "And there's lots of good schools besides Stanford. I won't be any trouble, Aunt Liz. You won't have to

64

drive me around—I'll ride the bus or take the train. I've got some cash stashed away."

I tried to say something, but she talked right over me. "Mom says I have to be invited. But she wants me to leave, I think. We're really—not getting along well right now." She ended with a gulp that might almost have been a sob.

I could sympathize. Amy is actually the only member of my family I feel close to. My parents have disapproved of me since I was twenty, which makes them less than pleasant companions. My sister and brothers resented my not living close enough to Denver to help in the care of my frail mother and cantankerous dad. My nephews have little to no interest in their spinster aunt. I was very fond of Amy, and the urge to help her was strong.

"The thing is, Amy, this isn't a good time." That was an understatement. Being the target of a gossip campaign was hard enough without adding Rita's death into the mix. "There are things going on—"

"I won't interfere. And Aunt Molly says Uncle Bill has frequent-flyer miles he never uses, so she's going to give me enough for a ticket. I've never flown before, do you realize that?"

"Many people have never flown before." Including me. I contemplated the wonder of getting from Denver to San Francisco in two hours instead of three days of hard driving—hard on Babe, at least.

"You don't understand, Aunt Liz. I have to get away." Usually she was levelheaded and sunny. But just then, Amy sounded downright hysterical. "I just can't be here with her right now. I hate her so much!"

Renee, Amy's mother, was often at loggerheads with

her daughter. Renee was not a sympathetic woman, and although she adored Amy, her love took the guise of constant nagging and worrying. If she'd agreed to let Amy come visit me, without insisting on coming along, it was a sure sign that she'd reached the end of her rope.

Amy waited, not saying anything. I capitulated.

"Okay. Come on out. But be prepared to work. I've got a lot of fall digging to do."

She didn't gush her delight, as I expected her to. "Thanks, Aunt Liz," she said, her voice small. "You'll never know what this means to me." She hesitated. "I'm going to get my plane reservation now. Can I call you back soon with the time?"

After Amy hung up, I reviewed the conversation and found it worrisome. I didn't feel equipped to cope with teenage needs and angst, and frankly didn't want to face any of it. But perhaps it wouldn't involve me. I'd provided a place of refuge for Amy before, and certainly I could respect her privacy in a way that seemed impossible for Renee to do. If my niece had had a painful love affair or flunked one of her accelerated classes, I wouldn't pry. Whatever it was, she couldn't be any worse off with me than in the bosom of my caustic family.

Since I had to wait for Amy's call back, I made myself at home. Drake's house is larger and in better shape than mine. The back door opens right into the big kitchen, which gleams with his collection of well-kept cookware. He'd replaced the appliances and cabinets a couple of months before, and added vinyl flooring embosssed to look like Mexican pavers, but much easier on the occasional dropped dish. Meticulous order prevailed. I liked that.

His telephone and answering machine were on a small desk near the door, along with neatly labeled binders of recipes, a messier one of phone logs, and a folder jammed full of scraps of paper that were in some mysterious way important. The answering machine's blinking light indicated a message. I do not like telephones, but I do like answering machines. They keep callers at a distance, they lessen the intrusion.

Drake keeps a notebook for recording my messages, as well as a log for his. Since I don't get that many messages, I assumed the one on his machine would go in Drake's log, not mine.

The message was for me, from Drake. He'd already heard about the contretemps at the garden.

"Dammit, Liz, you are some kind of trouble magnet. Don't go poking around into this one. I don't care if you know every person in that garden like the back of your hand. Just stay out of it and let Bruno do his job." He added, as an afterthought, "I miss you. I'll call at eight tonight."

Not a message I needed to write down. I reset the answering machine and put on the kettle to make tea. Drake has a supply of my homemade tea bags in a glass canister near his stove. He's a coffee man himself, though struggling to cut back his consumption. His chrome-laden Italian espresso machine didn't make that easier. In the evenings he'd froth up a bunch of milk for his decaf cappuccino and my hot chocolate. It seemed luxurious to me, to sit sipping our foamy drinks, watching a video if we were at his house, or talking about books in my living room. At times, I'd found it stifling, too. I had felt bad about the relief his departure for Seattle caused me, bad because his dad's illness was a cause of distress, not relief. And while I missed him, missed those creamy cups of conviviality, I also welcomed the quiet, the lack of demand.

Now Amy would come and shatter that. She would have to sleep in the middle of everything, on the lumpy old sofa bed in my living room. Her teenaged debris would be everywhere—hair equipment, makeup bags bulging with weird colors, jangly heaps of costume jewelry, jeans and T-shirts so frayed you would think them overdue for the ragbag. She did try to keep it all straight, but her definition of tidy and mine came from different dictionaries.

Waiting for the water to boil, I wandered through the living room. Drake's abrupt departure had caught his living room in its usual chaotic state. He limited his organizational efforts to the kitchen.

This was one reason why we often sat in my living room in the evening. Years of living in my VW bus have made me very sensitive to clutter. My house is small and I don't have a lot of stuff, so cleaning is a relatively simple process. Drake's living room overflows with stacks—books in teetering piles, videotapes in and out of cases, newspapers and journals piled on opposing ends of the coffee table, and a sofa draped with whatever he puts down on his way through the room—a shirt, a stack of files, a basketball, a towel.

Despite the peace and quiet I'd craved, I suddenly felt an overwhelming longing to see Paul lounging on the sofa—after having pushed all the junk down to one end.

The kettle whistled. I was pouring hot water on a tea bag of lemon balm and peppermint when Amy called back.

"I can be there tomorrow around noon. Is that okay?" Her voice was anxious.

"It's fast."

"I don't care how early I have to get up. It's worth it to get away from here."

"Amy, is something—going on, something I should know about? Because—"

"Don't worry, Aunt Liz." Her laugh was brittle. "Everything will be fine, once I get to California."

That sounded like famous last words.

# 9

"AMY'S a dear girl," Bridget said, passing me the bowl of green beans, "but should she be coming to visit just now? It's not a particularly good time, is it?"

She wasn't more specific about why it wasn't a good time because the three adults at the Montrose dinner table were outnumbered by the four children. Corky, the eldest at seven, had his ears pricked up under his blazing thatch of curly red hair. He passionately resented the unfairness of a world where adults could know things that children could not. He frequently managed to find out, and garble, any secrets he suspected his mom of keeping from him.

Sam, the next oldest at five, didn't care about the meaningless bibble-babble around him. He ate stolidly through a large helping of spaghetti before beginning on his salad. The garlic bread lay on his plate, untouched. He would eat it last. I knew his patterns because I'd minded the four Montrose offspring while Bridget and Emery had been in Hawaii not long before.

Mick, the youngest boy, had graduated at three to a booster seat on a regular chair. He loved the freedom of climbing up and down on his own during meals, and made use of it way too often for my delicate spinster nerves. Bridget was oblivious, however, and even Emery did no more than haul Mick back by his shirttail when he attempted to leave the room.

"Do you need a high chair again?" Emery spoke sternly when he plunked his son back into the booster seat, but his hand smoothing Mick's straight brown hair was tender. "We all sit at the table during meals. That includes you."

Mick looked at him thoughtfully. "Okay," he said at last. He rarely spoke in more than monosyllables, although Bridget had been assured by his preschool teacher that he had a perfectly adequate vocabulary when he needed it.

Moira was conducting an art project on the high chair tray, involving swirls of spaghetti and sauce, tastefully ornamented with garlic bread crumbs. She had been using her face as a palette to mix her materials. "More," she demanded. For a toddler, her voice was surprisingly strong.

"Not until you eat some," Bridget said. "How about a green bean?"

"No want." Moira's little mouth snapped shut.

"It's not a great time for Amy to visit," I said, keeping an eye on Corky, who was keeping an eye on me. "But she has an unexpected school holiday and she really, really wanted to get away. Renee's even agreeing to let her come. They must really be mixing it up lately."

Corky sucked up a few stray strands of spaghetti. "Is Amy gonna stay with you again? Is that what you're talking about?"

"She's coming for a few days."

"Cool!" He nudged Sam in the ribs. "Amy's coming. Did you hear that?"

"Amy with the purple hair?" Sam looked up from his plate. "She baby-sat us."

"She taught us that cool card game, remember? Seven-card stud," Corky said with relish. He helped another massive forkful of spaghetti into his mouth, rendering him speechless while he tried to contain it.

Bridget and Emery appeared unconcerned at this revelation of their offspring's corruption. Emery even smiled. "How's she doing with her stock market investing?" He leaned back, pushing the lock of red hair out of his eyes. In the past few months, I'd noticed more and more gray in his hair, though he wasn't forty yet. An aura of energy surrounded him, even when he was sitting down with tired-looking eyes. "She's quite the go-getter for a high school student. Girl's got a jump on her future already."

"I didn't ask her how the investing goes. She was pretty overwrought, really. That's why I couldn't say no." I met Bridget's worried gaze.

Corky had seized on the word *overwrought*. "She's not, like, rotting or anything?" His eyes were filled with dread.

"No, hon. It just means too emotional, like you get when you're tired and something happens that you don't like."

"Oh." Corky thought it over, stuffing in the last of his spaghetti. "CanIbescused?" He was sliding off his chair before Bridget nodded.

Sam followed him, and Mick, staring at his dad, said, "Me, too," and slid off the booster seat. Moira set up a screech.

Emery had to shout to make himself heard. "You boys wash your faces and hands before you touch anything, especially the TV."

At the sink, Bridget passed a washcloth ruthlessly over

Moira. She was done before Moira even started to howl about it. I marveled at this. When I tried, ever so gently, to wash her, she screamed like a banshee. Bridget's no-nonsense approach really seemed to work. She put the baby down, and Moira made a beeline for the living room.

Bridget finished rinsing out Moira's bib and came back to the table with the bottle of Merlot we'd been working on. "Here's to college," she said, topping off our glasses and lifting her own. "A mere sixteen and a half years until they're all gone."

"I won't last that long," Emery said. "What are they watching?"

"*Aladdin*. Should be okay." Bridget turned to me. "I didn't want to ask in front of Corky, but how are you doing? What have you heard since this morning?"

"I've heard nothing." I sipped the wine, admiring its dark, rich color. "However, Lois came to see me this afternoon. She's in a swivet."

I filled them both in on Lois's visit, and they agreed it was strange. "But not any stranger than someone getting killed at the garden," Emery added.

"Strange is one word for it." I shivered.

"Actually," Bridget said, "the gardeners aren't as bad as sports parents." She and Emery exchanged looks. "The soccer coach and a couple of the parents from that game last Saturday sounded like they were ready to start a rumble."

"It's the volunteer syndrome." Emery sounded like this continued some previously fought skirmish with his wife. "Like I said when that site council thing broke out, volunteers always get bent out of shape about something at any given point. They get into turf battles."

"Literally, in this case." Bridget topped up my glass. "I mean, most of the time the gardeners cooperate with each other. If your neighbors plant something tall that shades your plot, you tell them about it, and they don't do it the next season. But some people take sheer thoughtlessness as a hostile act and get themselves totally lathered up over it. The whole Bermuda grass thing—" She shrugged.

"But none of that is enough to kill over."

"I'm sure it will turn out to be a freak accident," Emery said in a soothing voice. "People who garden just aren't the kind of people who kill."

"All kinds of people garden," I said. "They're not all nice, by any means." I thought of Carlotta's round, sweet-looking face. She seemed so comfortable, until you noticed her mean little eyes.

"That's true," Emery said. "After all, Webster isn't my idea of a gardener." He drained his glass and leaned back in his chair. "He's such a funny guy."

"Funny-peculiar, Emery means." Bridget went over to the sideboard to cut slices of a toothsome-looking apple pie that had been calling to me all during dinner.

"He's a good worker," Emery amended. "When I have to bring him on board because we're slipping our deadlines, he really whips things out. But he wants us to jump through all these weird hoops—a dedicated phone line just for him, all kinds of security codes, have his check ready right there, not mailed to his P.O. box, et cetera. I don't really know where he lives."

"Maybe he's homeless." I knew the tricks to living without an address.

"Not with the rates he charges."

"He'd have no reason to do anything to Rita, either. I think they were dating at one time, but they seemed perfectly friendly to each other whenever I saw them." Bridget dealt us each a slice of pie. Its rich cinnamon aroma made my mouth water. "Tea?"

"Thank you." She poured me a cup of delicate green tea that somehow went perfectly with the apples. I savored my first bite, and said, "That's two men we've heard of in the past few hours that Rita was dating. I wonder if one of her boyfriends could have come to have it out with her, pushed her, and run away when he realized she was dead."

"It's not even that complicated," Emery insisted. "She must have tripped and fallen wrong. That rake across the path, maybe she didn't see it in time to avoid it. A dive into a foot-deep trench could be unhealthy."

Bridget's expression lightened. "That sounds reasonable. At any rate, Bruno will get to the bottom of it. He's very good at reading the crime scene."

Emery looked at her askance. "You're starting to sound like someone who spends hours watching TV cop shows."

"You know I don't," Bridget said indignantly. "They're too upsetting. I can't even watch those *Prime Suspect* shows you like."

"Children," I said. "Remember you are modeling the correct behavior here."

Emery smiled, but his voice was serious. "I don't want you ladies thinking of yourselves as sleuthhounds. Let the police take care of it. They know what they're doing."

"That's not what you said a couple of months ago

when all that proprietary code was leaked to your competitor. You said the police were idiots because they didn't find out who did it."

"Well, industrial espionage isn't really their bag." Emery waved that away. "This kind of accidental death looks pretty straightforward."

I had been thinking about it. "I'm not so sure it was an accident, Emery."

"Why not?" He didn't seem too happy to be contradicted, and I realized he didn't want Bridget to worry about it. But she was bound to worry, no matter what.

"Well, she couldn't have tripped on the rake. She fell backwards into the trench. If she'd fallen forward, she probably would have fallen on her head instead of her neck, and that might not have killed her."

He frowned. "I see what you're saying. But maybe she was backing up for some reason—to let someone by—"

"But anyone who was with her would have reported it right away," Bridget said. "If someone was there, they didn't speak up. That doesn't sound like an accident."

"Accident or not, let the police deal with it." Emery looked at each of us in turn. "They have the resources to figure it out. You don't."

"They don't know the garden, though," Bridget pointed out. "They don't know the gardeners. Not like we do."

"I don't know them so well, either." Now I found myself on Emery's side. "I've only been gardening there for four years, and you've been there less time than that, I believe. Tamiko has been there since it started in the seventies."

"You see?" Emery pushed his chair back. From the living room we could hear the frenetic strains of Robin

Williams singing about friendship. "I'm going to watch *Aladdin* with the kids. You coming?"

Bridget shook her head. "We still have to plan for Claudia's birthday party." The children in the living room shrieked with laughter, and she raised her voice.

"In fact, could you close the door?"

"Aren't we finished with the party?" I wouldn't have minded taking in a few minutes of *Aladdin* before I had to leave. My taste in movies is just about at the third-grade level.

Bridget watched the door swing shut behind Emery, then leaned forward, putting a hand on my wrist. "I don't want Emery to hear this," she murmured. "But I'm really afraid Rita's death was not accidental."

"What do you mean?" Her expression chilled me.

"Because I heard her arguing with someone just before I left this morning." Her eyes filled with tears. "I thought about going over and intervening, they sounded so nasty." She took a tissue from the box on the counter and blew her nose. "But I didn't. Maybe if I had, Rita would still be alive."

"It had nothing to do with you," I said, covering Bridget's hand with my own. "Why didn't you say something sooner?"

"I called Bruno, of course. I just didn't know if I should say anything about it to anyone else. You won't gossip. And I just felt you should know."

"Why? Who was arguing with Rita?"

"They were shouting at each other. Rita said that she had a right to do whatever she wanted. And *she* said—"

"She? Who?"

Bridget didn't answer that right away. "She said, 'Your rights may not last long, if you keep it up.' " Recounting this, Bridget shivered. "I'd never heard her sound mean like that. It gave me a chill."

"Who? Who was mean?"

Bridget looked at me with unhappy eyes. "Tamiko."

# 10

**WAITING** for Drake to call that evening, I couldn't settle down. I took his houseplants out onto the back porch for grooming, leaving the door open so I could hear the phone.

It was cold, with the damp, penetrating chill of winter nights in California. Some folks had their fireplaces going, adding the aroma of wood smoke to the air, along with the cold, fresh scent of redwood trees. The combination of wood smoke and redwood was nostalgic for me. Though I relished my comforts and my relative security, occasionally a longing for that other life, lived on more elemental terms with fewer complications, took me by surprise.

Finally the houseplants were ready for a bath in the kitchen sink. I carried them in, glancing at the clock. It was past Paul's usual hour to call, but his freedom to phone no doubt depended on what was happening with his dad at any given moment.

The house was too empty and quiet. I put on a CD, Ry Cooder's *Bop Til You Drop*. It was sufficiently raucous to fill the silence. While I was at it I straightened the couch, carrying the newspapers out to the recycling bin on the front porch.

I wouldn't even have noticed the car across the street if

the streetlight hadn't glinted on a fluffy white head in the driver's seat, bent at an angle over the steering wheel.

Enough weird stuff had been happening to send me into panic mode. I ran across the street. When I got close enough, I saw that the person in the car was not unconscious or hurt, just reading, with the streetlight's help. It was Carlotta.

I thought about turning around and going back inside. But the anger that had pushed me into confronting her in the garden was still alive inside me. I was tired of being a doormat for her Hush Puppy–shod feet.

I tapped on the car window next to her, and she jerked around to peer out.

"What are you doing here?" I didn't waste time on the preliminaries.

She rolled the window part of the way down, treating me to a bland smile. "Why, Liz. What do you mean? This is my old neighborhood, after all. Surely I can come back and park on the street for a little while."

"Considering the big deal you made about leaving because you felt unsafe, I'm surprised to see you sitting out here at night."

She tossed her head. "I'm just keeping an eye on your house in case anything should happen."

"Like what?" I noticed again how small her eyes really were beneath her makeup. And how cold.

"Like someone else dying," she said. "It would help to have a witness, don't you agree? I could help you out by giving you an alibi."

"I won't need an alibi. What I need is for you to leave me alone."

Triumph glinted in those little eyes. "I have only your

best interests at heart. Now that everyone's talking about how you're always around when people die—"

"You know, Carlotta, you are so brave." I stooped to be closer to her face. She shrank back. "After all, if I'm a cold-blooded murderer, a person might think twice before annoying me."

"I don't know what you mean." Her hand rested uneasily on the ignition key.

"Well, if I'm so dangerous, you're an idiot to be dogging me like this. And if you know I'm not dangerous, making it safe to go around whispering rumors, then you prove you don't really think I have anything to do with the deaths."

She puzzled that through for a moment. "You must have something to do with them. There never used to be so many murders in Palo Alto before you came around."

"That's a lie, too." I had had my own fears on that score, settled by cruising through the archives at the main library. "I've checked the newspapers. There are homicides every few months, and every time, the paper says how unusual it is for people to be killed in Palo Alto."

"There you have it," she said, triumphant again. "Even the newspapers, who always look for the worst things, say it's not usual."

"Well, have it your way. I'm a bad person. Now, who should be my next victim?" I held a finger up to my chin, thinking visibly. "Someone who's always bothering me. Who shoves herself in where she's not wanted. Who can't seem to mind her own business." I looked down at her face, pale in the streetlight. "Do you know anyone who fits that description?"

She gave a little scream. "Don't you dare threaten me!" But there was excitement in her voice, too. Her gaze slid sideways to the big handbag lying on the seat beside her.

As clearly as if she'd articulated it, I knew there was a tape recorder in that handbag. I, too, have carried a tape recorder around, and knowledge of its hidden mission has weighed heavily on me.

"And don't bother showing that tape around anywhere. I imagine my lawyer will have a lot to say about you trying to trap me into an admission of guilt. I'll have to remember to add that to the list of things I want to sue you for."

"Sue me?" She reared back. "You couldn't. You don't have any money."

"All the better reason to sue someone who does. For someone without money, a good name is even more valuable."

"No attorney would even talk to you."

"Tamiko's daughter will." I leaned closer. "Just leave me alone, Carlotta. Or it could cost you."

"You won't get away with this." She started her car, speaking over the engine noise. "People like you should be locked up before they do something bad."

"Now, is that slander? Or libel? I can never remember which. But I do know that it could be quite profitable—to me. Too bad I don't have a tape recording of you saying that."

Her hand rested possessively on the bag. "I don't know what you're talking about." She rolled up her window and roared away in her big Buick.

I went back into Drake's living room. The music met me, taking me by surprise, since I'd forgotten about putting it on. I thought about calling Bruno to fill him in on that surreal encounter. But I was expecting Drake's call, so I made a few notes of what Carlotta had said and wondered if I should talk to Tamiko's daughter after all.

After that was done I shelved a few books for Drake, and ended up sitting beside the telephone with his battered old copy of *The Black Arrow*. I was just getting into the War of the Roses when the phone rang.

"Sorry I'm late," Drake said when I answered. "Mom and I and Daphne went out for dinner with some family friends. It was good to get away from the hospital."

Daphne was his sister. I asked about his dad, and he told me a little about the situation. Medicine is, I suppose, very advanced and capable of saving us from untimely ends, but the procedures Frank Drake was going through sounded like high-tech torture. "They finished matching tissues," he ended. "Probably do the bone-marrow thing in the next couple of days."

"Will you be in the hospital, too, then?"

"God, I hope not." He sounded depressed. "The place is a total bummer. But it's weird to live at home again, too. My mom keeps asking me if I have any laundry for her to wash, and stuff like that. I feel a hundred years old at the hospital, and ten years old here."

"Poor old Drake." I hated hearing him so down. "Pretend I'm giving you a nice neck rub."

"If I'm going to pretend, I can do better than that." He paused. "So, about the death in the garden. I've gotten a few e-mails from Bruno."

"Rita. Quite a shock for the gardeners."

"You're not mixing it up, are you? Just hang back, Liz. Let Bruno do his job."

"I'm not hindering him. Actually, since I'm being stalked—"

"You're what?" That woke him up.

"Carlotta Houseman. For some reason, she's stalking me. Keeps showing up everywhere I go, whispering that I'm a murderer."

"That's actionable." He was quiet a moment. "This is Carlotta, that old bag from your writing workshop?"

"Right. What's that noise?"

The noise was Drake laughing. "Sorry, Liz. It must be unnerving. But I just can't feature an elderly stalker, especially that fluffy-looking grandma. I mean, really. How can she stalk you?"

"When she finally drives me over the edge, then you'll take it seriously, I suppose." I could understand his laughter. I wanted to join it, but something held me back. "What if she's so determined to make me look like a murderer that she starts killing people in my vicinity?"

"Hmm." Drake wasn't laughing anymore. "Not very likely, I'd say."

"She was parked in front of your house tonight, and she had a tape recorder going while we talked."

"Hmm."

"Is that all you can say?"

"Well, what do you want? I'll mention it to Bruno in my next e-mail. Just stay out of trouble, Liz. If that's possible."

"It's not," I said mournfully. "Amy's coming to visit."

"That'll be nice," he said, his voice cautious. "When? For Christmas break?"

"No. Tomorrow. Her school burned down or something, and she's fighting with Renee."

"She didn't burn the school down, did she?" He was laughing again. "No, don't get mad. I know she wouldn't do anything like that—probably. Well, you two girls have a good time."

"Maybe we'll start by having a garage sale. You've got a lot of junk around here."

Drake was quiet for a minute. "I miss you, Liz."

"I miss you, too."

He sighed. "I don't know how much longer this will take. I just wish—"

"Me, too," I said when he didn't finish.

His voice was rough. "I know you can get along without me. I just don't want you to enjoy it."

"No danger of that." My throat was clogging up with something. I knew I had to get off the line. "I'll see you soon."

"I'll call again tomorrow."

We hung up, and I had recourse to the box of tissues he kept in his bathroom before I went back to my own house, where the only love I got was from a large black and white dog who never told me to stay out of trouble. Maybe because Trouble was his middle name.

# 11

**SOMETHING** was very wrong with Amy. I had expected her to be exuberant at having gotten away from her mother, and with Amy, exuberant was a very high gloss on her normal bouncy, cheerful self.

Waiting at the end of the cordoned-off area where passengers ran the gamut of greeters like me, I watched her plod up the ramp and into the airport lounge. No bounce. No shine. Even her hair looked dull, if anything that orange could be deemed dull. The dark brown roots, about the color of my hair, were at least an inch long, another indicator of trouble. Instead of the ragged jeans and skimpy T-shirt I'd expected, she wore a baggy linen pinafore dress, with a faded jean jacket shrugged on over it. Her ancient carpetbag, the kind with wooden handles, bulged alarmingly. The whole effect was saved from waifdom only by Amy's extremely well-endowed bosom, undisguisable even in the pinafore.

"Aunt Liz." She smiled when she saw me, but the smile wrung my heart, so beset with worries did it seem. She probably didn't realize how much of what she felt showed—life hadn't yet dealt her the poker face that keeps the world at bay.

"Hey, Amy. Was the flight good?"

"Not so good." She swallowed. "Lost my pretzels in a major way."

"Do you want to hit the bathroom?"

"That would be fine." She looked a little wobbly. Maybe airsickness was all that ailed her.

"So, flying isn't so hot after all?" I leaned one hip on the counter and watched her wash up.

She was teenager enough to glance around and make sure no one was staring at the novice flyer. "Well, it was pretty exciting," she admitted. "And scary, too. I kept imaging all the stuff that could go wrong. I was, like, let me off! But then it was cool for a while, until we were crossing the Yosemite mountains."

"The Sierra," I said.

"Yeah. The Sierras, or whatever. It got bumpy then." She shivered and splashed a little extra water on her face. I realized she wore no makeup, another major style change. "Anyway, I'm here. Really fast, too. It's much better than riding the hound." She smiled, though wanly, at my puzzled expression. "Taking a Greyhound bus," she explained. "I don't mind hurling if it saves so much time."

"I'm glad you're here." I picked up the carpetbag. It weighed a ton. "Let's get the rest of your luggage."

"That's all." She wrested it away from me, and I let her. "I didn't bring anything else."

We chatted about family stuff on the way to the parking garage. Amy exclaimed with rapture over Barker, who erupted out of the bus when she opened the side door. "Such a big boy! Such a good boy!" He writhed his happiness, licking her hands, and when she grabbed him around the neck, her face. Then she straightened guiltily. "I know, Aunt Liz. Not allowed."

"Only in greeting or parting," I agreed.

She ordered Barker back into the bus, slung in her carpet-bag, and climbed up into the passenger seat. "Babe looks good," she remarked. Amy was responsible for the name Babe; she'd christened my bus during her last visit.

"Just got her 225,000-mile oil change," I bragged. I admit to pampering the bus in terms of oil and timing adjustments, which I've learned to do myself. So far, the pampering has worked. Buying a replacement vehicle would empty my savings account.

Amy fell silent as I pulled onto 101. Conversation in Babe is difficult anyway, due to the roaring.

We were almost to Palo Alto before she spoke. "Thanks for letting me come, Aunt Liz." She gripped my arm for a minute, then went back to petting Barker, who stood between the two front seats as I drove, nudging Amy whenever her hand stopped its attentions.

"I'm just glad to see you." I didn't say anything about Rita's death. With any luck, it would be cleared up before Amy even knew it had happened. "A very dramatic way to get a holiday."

"No kidding," Amy muttered. She closed her eyes and leaned her head back.

"Do you feel bad, still? Do you need something in your stomach?" I stole glances at her, slackening my already stately pace a bit. "We'll be home in less than ten minutes. Should I stop?"

"Aunt Liz. I'm okay." She gave me a shaky smile. "Just leftover airsickness, I guess. Maybe it would help to eat something. Are there crackers in the emergency kit?"

I reached between the passenger seat and the sink that faces backward behind it, and pulled out the plastic container that's meant to tide me over in case an earthquake strands me in Babe someday.

Amy rooted around in the shallow bin, finding a package of peanut butter crackers, which Bridget buys for me at Costco, making them the only packaged snack I can afford. By the time we pulled into my drive, the crackers were gone and she looked better.

"I got some stuff for lunch," I told her, unlocking the front door. "Real food, I mean."

Amy grinned and headed for the refrigerator, an automatic teenage response that appears to be triggered by coming into any house, anywhere. "Look, pre-sliced cheese! Wow! And mayo, too!"

"I remember what you like." Amy's taste in food was, in my opinion, horrid. She did join me in cherry tomatoes and baby carrots from my garden. And she drank a big glass of the gallon of milk I had gotten instead of my usual half gallon. I make granola for myself, but remembering how much cereal Amy could put away in one sitting, I had bought an enormous box of Cheerios for her, which she started on directly after her thick cheese sandwich.

Putting down her glass and taking an absent swipe at the resulting milk mustache, Amy gazed around the kitchen. "It's good to be back," she said, with a contented sigh. "Aunt Liz, is it possible to be poor and happy? Don't you hate not having enough money for things you want?"

I blinked under this unexpected attack. "I don't know, Amy. I always feel so lucky just to have a house to live in. And lately I've made enough writing to keep from having to do temp work. That's about as good as it gets in my life."

89

Her lips twisted. "You're not helping."

"What would help?"

"It would help," Amy said, slumping in her chair, "if you told me I would never be happy unless I got a good education and earned enough money to give myself a good life—not like Aunt Molly, who has everything but feels bad because Uncle Bill does all the providing. And not like Mom, who has to ask Dad for everything and take what she gets. I want to get it for myself—everything! I want to travel. I want to feel important. I want to pick up the phone and order myself the things I want, the things I worked for!" She halted the tirade, drawing in a deep breath.

"Well, okay."

"Huh?" She focused on me instead of her inner vision.

"Sounds like a plan. What's holding you back?"

She wouldn't look at me again. Instead she stacked her cereal bowl, sandwich plate, and glass and took them to the sink.

"Aunt Liz, are you still Catholic?"

I realigned my mind. "I'm getting confused here, Amy."

"I mean, do you go to confession, and all? Do you go to mass?"

"Not for a long time." Not since the middle of my disastrous marriage, which had shown me the kind of mercy a patriarchal religion reserves for its daughters. "I've sort of evolved my own religion. Gardening is one of its central rites."

She smiled, but it didn't last long. "I don't know what to do. I'm in terrible trouble."

It all came together for me, finally. I felt very dumb not to have seen it coming. "You're pregnant."

Amy heaved one great, shuddering sigh. "Oh, Aunt Liz." Her voice broke, and then she was crying.

I got up and put my arm around her, guided her back to her chair. I put the kettle on and got out the chamomile tea. If ever there was an occasion that called for soothed nerves, this was it.

Finally she stopped sobbing. I fished my clean bandanna out of my pocket and gave it to her, and she mopped up and accepted the cup of tea.

"It's such a relief to be able to tell someone," she said, her voice still quivering with emotion. "I couldn't tell Mom. She would hit the roof. And Dad—I can't imagine."

I could, only too well. "It would be epic," I agreed. "But—does this mean you're not going to tell them?"

"I don't know." Amy used the hankie again, then squared her shoulders. "It's my problem. I'm going to decide what to do. Then maybe I'll tell them."

I didn't know what to say. Amy would be a pariah in the Sullivan clan if any of them knew. I didn't feel that I could encourage her to keep her parents in the dark, though. Maybe we were denying Andy and Renee the chance to show their magnanimous sides.

Nah.

"So, are you thinking abortion?" It seemed like a good idea to get everything on the table.

"Of course I am." Amy stared at me. "It's the first thing I thought about when I suspected. I don't want to have a baby. I wasn't trying to have a baby."

"What were you trying to do?" She frowned, and I added hastily, "If you don't mind my asking."

"You won't believe it." She stared into her teacup. "I sort of told Tiffany. I mean, I didn't say it was me. I just said I heard it happened to someone, and she couldn't stop laughing. No one would ever believe it, even it it's in Ann Landers all the time."

"Why don't you tell me and let me see?"

Amy looked up at me, her chin thrust out. "I was at a party at this guy's house I didn't know very well. There were a bunch of jocks there, which isn't my scene really. But my friend Amber and I had decided we would get drunk, not really drunk, but drunk enough to see what it was like, and we knew there'd be booze at this party because the jocks always get booze. So Amber and I bagged a couple of beers and went to the sunroom. It was a really nice house, and there was a hot tub in the sunroom, and after we had the beers we got in—with our underwear on, you know. Everyone had their underwear on. A couple of the other girls went off with a couple of the boys, and Amber and I had another beer, and I got kind of sleepy. Next thing I knew, it was dark and Amber was gone and this jerky boy was putting the moves on me." Her lower lip trembled. "He had my panties off and was humping on me—like Barker does to people's legs sometimes—but right on top of me."

"Oh, Amy. He was raping you?"

"He didn't get that far. I grabbed his balls and told him to stop bothering me or I'd make him a eunuch." She shook her head, scorn dripping from her voice. "He didn't even know what that meant, for Pete's sake. Anyway," her eyes slid away, "he came right there, like he couldn't help himself, and then he scrambled out. He was such a moron! I wouldn't have his baby if the future of the human race depended on it!"

"So that was it? He didn't—penetrate?"

"No." She added reluctantly, "He was a total loser. But

to be fair, I probably looked like a slut. I can't really blame it all on him."

"But you didn't get help? No one else saw?"

"It didn't seem like that big a deal, and there weren't any witnesses, so what was the use of talking about it? Besides," she added, "I couldn't find my panties, and I didn't want to get out without them on, because after he left, other people came into the room. I was sitting there, groping around the hot tub with my toes, trying to find my panties."

With a supreme effort I kept my face straight. "I hope you did find them eventually."

"I didn't. But Amber brought me a towel." Her lips twisted. "And just because of that I get pregnant. It's not fair. I wasn't even really misbehaving. Why should I have to pay such a heavy price?"

"You could have the baby and give it up for adoption."

She shook her head stubbornly. "I'm not going to school pregnant. I'm not going through all the whispering and the questions. Do you think that jerk would even acknowledge it was his? It would all be on me. Mom, Dad—Gramma and Grampa would all croak." She stared at me, wide-eyed. "Is that what it was like for you?"

"No, but it wasn't pleasant. And, as it turned out, they were right to tell me not to marry him."

"They would make me have the baby," Amy said with conviction, "and I would die."

"You wouldn't die. But I agree that you're old enough to decide for yourself what to do." I watched her nervous fingers pat the bread crumbs on the table. "How pregnant are you?"

"Less than two months." Amy hugged herself. "I have to decide soon."

So she hadn't really made up her mind yet.

"Well," I said, refilling her milk glass, "as long as you're eating for two, I'll get out the apple pie Bridget sent me home with last night."

# 12_____

**AMY** ate more than half of the little pie and seemed to feel better. I, however, could not be comforted by apples, even with lots of cinnamon. The ramifications of Amy's pregnancy chased everything else out of my brain. "Man," I muttered, getting up to carry plates to the sink, "Renee would—"

"You've got to swear, Aunt Liz." Amy jumped out of her chair and grabbed my arm. "You've got to solemnly promise that you will never, never tell Mom, no matter what. You've got to, Aunt Liz."

Her mouth was stubbornly set, her eyes brilliant with command. For a moment I saw my father in her, the rigid, controlling man who wanted us all to dance to his piping. Then tears filmed those sharp eyes, and she was just Amy, desperate with trouble.

I loosened her grip on my arm and patted her hand. "Amy, hon, I can't promise that. You can't tie my hands before we know all the circumstances. What if there were complications and you ended up in the hospital? Don't you see the position you're putting me in here?"

She wasn't listening. Tears rolled down her cheeks. Her head came to rest limply on my shoulder. "They can't know. I can't tell them now, maybe not ever! You've got to help me!"

I guided her into the living room. "You're so tired, Amy. Why don't you try to take a little nap? I won't tell anyone anything you don't want me to. Rest now. Then we'll talk."

She let me tuck the afghan around her shoulders, nestling her head into the pillow I'd put together from unpieced quilt squares left in the closet after my friend Vivien's death. Barker assumed his Sphinx position on the rag rug beside the couch, until he saw me put on my garden shoes. He sprang to attention, prancing out the door before me.

We went around the raised beds, tending the baby veggies. I pulled enough carrots and little beets for dinner, then added some more, remembering Amy's appetite. I also cut the small ruby leaves of kale, and the baby spinach and mustard greens. Whatever she did about her maternal dilemma, Amy had to eat properly.

Bridget stopped by just as I finished plucking a few ripe cherry tomatoes off the browning vines. She was wearing that vertical line between her eyebrows, the one that indicated worry. "Where's your young visitor?" she asked, glancing around the yard.

I remembered her concern when she heard Amy was coming. "You guessed Amy was pregnant, didn't you?"

"So she is? God, I hoped I was wrong." Bridget sank onto the edge of the raised bed. "You certainly don't need this."

"Neither does Amy."

Bridget pressed her lips together. "Amy did the deed, so she should take responsibility. And if she needs help, she should go to her parents for it, not you."

It was a little surprising to hear Bridget speak so sternly; she usually bends over backward to give people the benefit of the doubt. Part of me agreed with her. Part of me felt put upon by having to cope with Amy's troubles. But in this particular case, I didn't think Bridget's poor opinion of my niece was deserved.

"It wasn't as much her fault as you might think." I spoke cautiously, not knowing how much of the story was mine to reveal.

"Oh, no. She wasn't raped, was she?" Bridget looked aghast. "Oh, how could I say such mean things? Poor Amy."

"No, no. She wasn't raped. Not technically. Not in any way that seems to bother her."

"Liz, if you think you're reassuring me—"

I tried not to say anything, but it popped out regardless. "Hot tub."

For a moment, Bridget looked blank. "You mean—"

I nodded. "Evidently it happens a lot. Amy said people write Ann Landers about it."

We stared at each other, faces solemn. Bridget spoke, her lips barely moving. "Is she watching?"

"She's asleep."

Her jaw began to quiver, and finally I could stand it no longer. We burst into laughter simultaneously, smothering the whoops and giggles as best we could against each other's shoulders. From a distance it must have seemed that two women were crying and consoling each other.

Bridget was the first to recover. "I feel terrible for doing that," she gasped, wiping her eyes.

"I feel much better." I reached for my bandanna and realized I'd left it with Amy, already sodden with female emotional collapse. "But I know what you mean. It's so hard to have to make this kind of choice knowing that people are trying not to laugh."

"It's no laughing matter." Bridget sobered completely. "She's thinking about an abortion?"

"My family is Catholic, you know." I wanted Bridget to understand why Amy dragged her troubles to my doorstep, like a cat with a dead mouse. "And Amy already doesn't get along well with her parents."

"Then they all really need counseling." Bridget's voice was gentler, but adamant. "Unless she's in physical danger from them, she should give them a chance to help her. They might surprise her."

"I said that, too." I picked up my basket. "But the thing is, I can see her point. I wouldn't want to tell them I was pregnant, knowing my brother, my dad. They're so proud of Amy's grades, and she's the only granddaughter. Renee would probably be on Amy's side, but she would feel compelled to tear a few strips off her verbally first."

"Well, I do feel for her." Bridget sighed. "Especially since she didn't really ask for it. And birth control can fail, as I personally know. It's just too bad anytime a baby isn't cause for celebration."

We ambled toward the house, Bridget stopping to smell the roses. "Why don't my flowers ever look this good? All I have is dead sticks," she complained.

"You stopped watering too soon. We haven't had enough rain for that. Besides, I gave the whole garden a big nutritious mulching in late August. This is the thanks I get." I dug the shears out of my apron pocket and cut off a spray of Margaret Merrill, a rose I think particularly appropriate for Bridget. "I'll put this in a milk carton or something and you can carry it home. Where's your little helper, anyway?" It suddenly occurred to me that Moira was nowhere to be seen.

Bridget buried her face in the creamy blooms. "Mmm—fragrant, too. Emery's doing the dad thing this afternoon while I go Christmas shopping."

"Isn't it early for that?"

"No." Bridget shuddered. "Already it's monstrously crowded at that big warehouse toy store, a place I hate so much that every time I go, I vow I won't go back. I ended up at the Sport and Toy downtown, paying a lot more. But you know, they had everything the boys wanted, stuff the other place was already out of."

"It seems to me that what those boys want changes almost daily. What if they outgrow Nerf before Christmas?"

"A risk I'll have to take." Bridget shrugged. "I'm getting burned out on the whole present thing. We're going to make stuff for everyone else in the family."

When we went inside, Amy was up, standing by the kitchen sink with a glass of milk in her hand. She greeted Bridget with pleasure, and I was relieved that Bridget didn't lecture. I got an empty milk carton out from under the sink and filled it with water for Bridget's roses.

"Aunt Liz," Amy said, staring out the window over the sink, "who is that woman? She's been watching your driveway ever since I got up."

I glanced out the window, not too surprised to see Carlotta's Buick parked at the end of the drive. "She's a nutty woman who's stalking me. No big deal."

Bridget was shocked. She joined me at the sink. "It's Carlotta," she exclaimed. "What in the world—you say she's stalking you?"

I was sorry I'd spoken so. It was beginning to seem funny to me, although the sight of her did send a bit of chill along my spine. "She's watching me. Thinks I'll mur—thinks I'll misbehave, I guess."

"The hag," Bridget muttered. "I'll speak with her on my way home."

"Are you going?" Amy had overlooked my slip, which was good, since I didn't want to have to go into all that right now. "I was wondering—could I talk to you for a little while, Mrs. Montrose?"

"Why, certainly, Amy." Bridget shot me a glance, but I didn't look at her. "Shall we walk around Liz's garden?"

I had hoped Amy would consult with someone more fitting to advise her than a spinster aunt. Bridget was that someone, as far as I was concerned. Despite her hard-line stance earlier, I knew she would do her best to give Amy an impartial viewpoint. I went to my desk to get my work in order, but with Amy temporarily out of the way, my thoughts returned to Carlotta, to Lois, to Tamiko. A picture of Rita, awkwardly disposed in Lois's garden plot, rose in my mind, and I remembered what Lois had said about her sainted Sidney. I wondered if Bruno knew about Lois's shrine.

Bridget and Amy came back. Amy looked subdued; she'd been crying. Bridget gave her a sympathetic pat. "I'm sorry, hon. I would like to help you make up your mind, but I can't. You've got to do this one on your own, unless your family—"

"You don't understand. No one understands." Amy headed for the bathroom, the only private refuge in my little house.

Bridget looked troubled. Then she turned to me. "I almost forgot what I really came over for. There's a memorial thing for Rita tonight at the garden. People have been putting flowers and candles there where she was found, and there's going to be some kind of brief ceremony. I'll stop by for you."

"I don't want to go." Thinking about the looks, the whispering, made me cringe.

"You should, though. Don't let the whisperers have power over you, Liz. I'll stick by you, and I know Tamiko will, too." A shadow crossed her face when she mentioned my garden neighbor. "She'll need your support as well. We'll prop each other up."

I surrendered, reluctantly. "Okay, I'll go. But if it's horrid, I may have to bolt."

"Understood." She took her milk carton of roses and left. I stood at the sink, scrubbing a couple of winter squash for baking, and saw her stop by Carlotta's car on her way to her own car. Bridget's shoulders slumped when she turned away after speaking to Carlotta. I felt like slumping, too. From the bathroom came the sound of Amy's gusty sobs.

I turned my back on the view of Carlotta parked at the end of my drive and put a pot of water on the stove. Then I went to my desk. Even if I wasn't really getting anything done, I could pretend I was working. There was some comfort in that.

# 13

NO matter what her state of mind, Amy's appetite remained unimpaired. She devoured a large quantity of pasta with vegetables, and most of an acorn squash. I had taken a loaf of zucchini bread from the freezer, and she ate that, too, spread with the cream cheese and honey mixture I make up and keep for a treat. She polished it all off with quantities of milk, and seemed more relaxed. I hoped I could afford to feed her for the next couple of weeks.

"That was good," Amy complimented me. "I'm thinking of being a vegetarian, Aunt Liz. Mom cooks so much meat all the time. It's oppressive."

"I'm only a vegetarian for economic reasons," I reminded her. "And you probably need to eat meat right now. I don't know much about pregnancy, but aren't you making a lot more red blood cells or something?"

"I don't care." Amy's jaw set mulishly. "I won't be pregnant for long, anyway." She sighed. "I think."

I wanted to ask what course of action she planned to follow, but I didn't. There was nothing she could do until Monday. Then I hoped to persuade her to see a doctor. She looked perfectly healthy, but it was best to be sure.

"God," she went on. "If only he wasn't such a jerk. It would be so wrong to allow his spawn to populate the world."

"Maybe the baby would take after you."

"And be a total idiot?" She laughed, shortly. "No, thanks." She looked down at herself. "Besides," she said, the words bursting out, "it's just too creepy. Like an alien force, invading my body. Changing everything. Would you believe my boobs could get any larger? And yet they did. Yuck! And other stuff happening, too."

"Did you get morning sickness?" I stacked her plate with mine.

She took the plates from me. "I'll wash the dishes. You made dinner, after all. And I'll do my share, Aunt Liz. You won't regret taking me in." She carried the dishes over to the sink, and I followed her with our glasses. "Yeah," she went on, picking up the last conversation but one, just like the White Queen, "I hurled a bit—that's what tipped me off. And now I have this strange feeling in my guts. I just want to go back to how things used to be. And I'm never going to even look at another guy for as long as I live!" She scrubbed the plates with violent thoroughness.

I rinsed and wiped, trying to be sympathetic without committing myself. "Won't Renee expect you to call and say you got here okay?"

"Good idea." Amy glanced around. "Did you finally get a phone?"

"No. But Drake's away, so we can use his."

"You mentioned he was gone." She looked at me. "For good?"

"I don't think so." While we walked across the lawn, I

told her about Drake's dad. It was half past five, way too early for him to call. And if I went to the memorial for Rita at the garden, I might miss his call anyway.

Amy spoke briefly to her mother, and then handed the phone to me. I hadn't expected that, or I wouldn't have been standing around Drake's kitchen, waiting for Amy to finish her call.

Renee was her usual grumpy self. "I don't know what ails that child," she said, with no preliminary niceties. "But I'm counting on you to talk some sense into her, Liz."

"I don't know any."

She snorted. "Don't give me that." There was a pause, and she spoke again. "Is—do you think—has she said anything?"

"She's enjoying her unexpected holiday." Amy's eyes were on me, silently demanding, pleading for, my complicity. "Barker's delighted to see her."

"She's standing right there, I suppose." Renee sighed into my ear. "Well, maybe you can call me when she's not there. I know there's something behind all this. If she's in trouble—"

"I have to go, Renee. We'll keep you posted."

Amy needed no urging to leave. I saw there were messages on the phone, but I didn't linger to check them out. Renee might call back, and there was no point in verbally dueling with her.

We went back to my house through the deepening dusk. Barker was restless, and Amy volunteered to take him for a walk.

"I'm going out for a while," I told her. "Bridget's coming to pick me up."

"That's okay. I'll just hang around after I get back and read or something." Amy patted my shoulder. "Don't feel you have to entertain me. I know I'm butting in here, and I won't be any trouble."

"You're not any trouble." I gave her a hug. "I wouldn't go to this thing, but Bridget thinks I should."

"Is it a party?" Amy looked speculative.

I shook my head. "Memorial service, sort of. For someone who died."

"Oh." She lost interest.

When Bridget arrived a few minutes later, she brought a book with her.

"In case you're interested," she said, handing it to Amy. "About pregnancy and birth. You should know both sides before you make up your mind."

"I guess." Amy took the book reluctantly. "You two have fun, if you can."

Bridget was driving Emery's car, a middle-aged Honda that was nevertheless luxurious by my standards, and by hers, since her regular vehicle was a rusty Suburban. She glanced at me while she started it up. "How's it going, anyway?"

"Renee suspects. We talked to her earlier. I think she's following a 'don't ask, don't tell' policy."

"Hmph." Bridget charged onto Middlefield. "I hope I never get into that position with Moira. It would break my heart if she was in trouble and wouldn't come to me."

"It's pretty common, though."

"Are you taking Amy to the doctor tomorrow?"

"I'm not taking her anywhere." Bridget started to speak, but I interrupted her. "As you pointed out, I'm not her mom. She's not my responsibility. If she wants a ride somewhere and it's important, I'll give her one, but I won't herd her around."

Bridget glanced at me skeptically. "Right. So you aren't going to see that she goes to a clinic?"

"I left the phone book open to Planned Parenthood on the kitchen table," I admitted, coming down from my moral high horse. "But you don't understand, Bridget. Amy's here because she wants to do something about it. If she was going to stick her head in the sand, she could do that in Denver."

"True enough." Bridget shook her head. "You read all these stories in the newspaper about girls who have babies without anyone in their families knowing they were pregnant—including themselves, evidently. So sad."

"Well, Amy's in charge. She'll handle it. I see my role as support person and hand-holder."

"You're very wise for someone who's never been a parent, Liz." Bridget turned onto Channing.

"It's easier to be objective from the outside," I said. "If I had children, I'd be just as irrational with them as any parent."

Bridget opened her mouth, then closed it again. I knew the question she wanted to ask, but she respected my privacy too much to ask it.

"I won't ever have children, Bridget." I looked at her in the glow of the instrument panel. "I know it seems immature and childish to you to duck that kind of commitment. But I can't have them, and I'm not exactly sorry. I wasn't cut out to be a mom."

Bridget looked as if she were bursting with questions, but at last, she just shrugged. "Oh, well. Maybe Amy will give you her baby."

She concentrated on pulling into the parking lot, while I sat, utterly silenced by the conviction that when I let Amy come to visit me, I'd gotten in way over my head.

# 14 _____

IT was full dark when we got out of the car and walked toward the garden. A pallid crescent of moon low in the sky gave little light. The surrounding trees filtered the glare from streetlamps along Embarcadero and by the library. The darkness was lively with people, however. They shone flashlights on each other and spoke in low voices. An occasional laugh broke the hush.

Bridget and I followed a couple of women along the perimeter path. I didn't recognize them, but they were talking about Rita, and their voices came back to us plainly. "I heard she was in an abusive relationship," one of the women said.

The other woman snorted. "If so, she was the abuser. I've known her since her mother married Jack Dancey. Nobody ever put anything over on that girl. The scenes she made! I tell you, it's a wonder someone in the family didn't kill her before now."

The first woman seemed to feel aggrieved that her nugget of gossip was dismissed. "Well, that's not what I heard. I heard that she and the youngest Dancey boy were quite an item at one time."

Her companion was silent a moment. "That's true," she said grudgingly. "But it didn't last long, and no one in the family liked it. After all, Rita made such a point of being a Dancey, using the family name, wanting everything Jack's boys had. It seemed almost incestuous that she and Tom should date."

"She'd date anything that moved," the first woman declared. By now Bridget and I had closed in on the two women in a shared wish to hear every detail of their conversation, but they didn't notice. "I heard she went out with several of the men gardeners, even married ones!"

"Well, she's dead now, poor thing," the other woman said with belated charity. "It's a blessing, really, that her mother didn't live to see this. She died of breast cancer a couple of years ago. Jack was devastated, but perhaps it was all for the best. Angela just doted on her daughter."

The women fell silent as we came to the area of fence near Lois Humphries's garden plot. A large crowd had gathered outside the garden there. Among them I saw several people I knew, including Webster Powell, who paid no attention to me, and a few other gardeners whose glances slid off when I encountered them. Carlotta stood near the fence. No one was talking to her, either. Evidently news of our scene in the garden the day before had spread.

The boards Lois had wanted used as fencing were still in a pile on the ground—all but one of them, which had been set across two upturned buckets, forming a makeshift altar. This was crowded with candles, tall ones as well as votives, and surrounded by bunches of flowers. Behind it the old wire mesh fencing had been roughly nailed onto the new uprights I had dug holes for, keeping the crowd away from Lois's plot.

Bridget stepped through the crowd, brushing past Webster, to add the candles she'd brought, lighting them from the other flames. I handed my flowers to her, and she placed them with those already there.

Then she rejoined me at the back of the crowd, letting others add their contributions. "Boy," she whispered. "Candles can really put out the heat. You can feel it all the way out here."

"They make a surprising amount of light." The candles gave a soft glow to that whole area of the garden. Behind the fence, the caution tape fluttering around Lois's plot was clearly visible. Also visible was Lois herself, frowning as she stood in the path next to the tape. She clutched something to her chest; at first I thought it was her ubiquitous clipboard, but the shape was different, more like a box.

"I guess the police investigation isn't over yet," Bridget said. "That's why they've set this up outside the fence. I thought it was going to be where Rita was found."

The woman in front of us turned around, revealing herself as Tamiko, her round face impassive. "Lois didn't want it in her plot. Said it would be a desecration."

We exchanged looks, our faces made dark and mysterious by the flickering light.

"Why did she say that?" The voice behind me made me jump.

"Oh, hi, Bruno." Bridget looked past me. I turned to see Bruno Morales standing in the path. "I didn't know you'd be here."

"As you say, we are still investigating. Why is Mrs. Humphries so angry at the dead woman?"

"I don't think she's angry, Detective Morales." Tamiko's voice was level. "She just didn't want a shrine constructed on her garden plot."

"I can understand that." Bruno moved closer. "But why is she concerned with desecration?"

"She's kind of nutty." Bridget glanced around before imparting this in a low voice. "Obsessive."

Tamiko looked at Bridget, then at Bruno. "It's more than that. Her husband's ashes are kept there. In effect, it's already a shrine."

Bridget took a moment to absorb that.

"It's true," I said. "She told me yesterday afternoon."

Bruno took out a pocket notebook and a tiny penlight, and made a note. Bridget nudged me.

"Webster sure doesn't look heartbroken."

Webster was talking with another gardener, and judging from his smile, he didn't have a care in the world.

Bruno jumped on Bridget's remark. "Why should he be heartbroken?"

"We heard some gossip on the way from the parking lot," Bridget told him. "These women were saying that Rita dated her stepbrother, Tom Dancey, and one of them said she dated anything that moved, including some of the men gardeners. I remembered then that she and Webster went out for a while." She looked at Tamiko. "You know, Tamiko. It was when he planted raspberries between your plot and his, and you asked Rita to make him get rid of them because it was against the rules to plant anything invasive, including raspberries. And she didn't. You told me then that they were involved and that's why she let him get away with it."

"I really don't remember," Tamiko said deliberately, and moved away.

"Why would she say that? She was really upset about it at the time," Bridget said, staring after Tamiko.

Bruno made another note. "I would like to ask a favor

of both of you," he began. Then a tall man standing next to the altar began to speak to the crowd. The authority in his voice quieted everyone, even Bruno.

"Thank you all for coming tonight. I'm Tom Dancey, Rita's brother. Rita would have appreciated your concern. She loved her work in the garden, and looked forward to a long and happy association here. This senseless accident had been difficult for her family to accept." He paused and shaded his eyes.

"He must be the brother who was romantically involved with her," Bridget whispered. When Tom Dancey didn't speak for a few minutes, other people in the crowd began whispering, too. I saw the two ladies we had followed from the parking lot exchange significant glances.

"Someone from the police department would like to say a few words," Tom Dancey went on, mastering his emotion. "Once more, thank you for this beautiful display of affection. Rita would have been proud. Maybe she is proud, somewhere."

There was a sympathetic murmur from the crowd. I waited for Bruno to go forward, but it was Officer Rhea who stood in front.

"We deeply regret that we are not quite finished with our investigation," she said. "As Mr. Dancey said, all the evidence points to accident. But in case it was not an accident, we are doing a very thorough check of the scene. And we'd like to ask all of you to let us know if you remember anything suspicious, or if anything in the least bit out of the way catches your eye in the next few days. I would be glad to give my card to anyone who wants it, or you can reach us through the police dispatcher. Please don't hesitate to call or to come and talk to me if you have any concerns."

The crowd began to break up. A few people went to talk to Tom Dancey; a few more headed for Officer Rhea.

Bruno cleared his throat, looking from Bridget to me. "As I said, I have a favor to ask."

"That depends," Bridget said warily. "I've told you everything I know, and a lot more besides. What else do you need?"

"I need you to go around the garden with me and tell me about the gardeners." Bruno smiled easily. "Nothing for the record, just to let me get acquainted with them. I feel that the personalities of the people involved are important."

"So you are sure it wasn't an accident." Bridget sounded distressed.

"No, I am not sure. That is why I need more information. The case is obscure right now. And the more time that goes by, the less likely we are to find out what really happened. Will you help me?"

"Does it have to be tonight?" I wanted to get back—to check on Amy, I told myself, though I knew it was more to do with Drake's phone call.

"Tomorrow morning would be okay." Bruno whipped out another little book, this one an agenda of some kind. "If you could meet me here?"

"I have to do snacks at preschool," Bridget said. "It would have to be after ten—eleven would be better."

"And I'm probably taking Amy to the doctor first thing in the morning. Eleven would work better for me, too."

"Good." Bruno made a note. "Thank you both. I feel sure that with your excellent skills of observation, you will help me understand all this better."

"Well, guess I'd better get home now." Bridget started back along the perimeter path, and I followed her.

Bruno came along with us. "Have you heard from Paolo lately?" He looked at me, his dark eyes liquid in the faint moonlight.

"He's left a couple of messages on his answering machine," I said cautiously. Everyone persisted in treating me as if I were Drake's special friend. Maybe that was true. But I didn't like my personal life being known by so many people.

"I had e-mail from him today." Bruno smiled. "He instructs me to refrain from upsetting you at the same time he says not to drag you into it. I am not trying to drag you in, Liz. But I must ask questions, and I believe both you and Bridget can help me with background."

Bridget looked uncertain. We had reached her car, and she stood by the driver's door, keys in hand. "So can other gardeners, who've been here a lot longer."

He spoke patiently. "Those other gardeners might not be such careful observers. Be assured I plan to talk to many of them, especially any who feel they have something to tell me. But I ask you and Liz for your points of view because I respect your abilities. If Paolo were here, I'd let him handle this. But he may not be back for a long time. Maybe not ever."

The last words were spoken low. As soon as they were out of his mouth, Bruno looked as if he would like to call them back.

I could say nothing. I felt a great hollowness in my chest, and the lump in my throat would have kept any words from getting out.

Bridget was not so handicapped. "What do you mean by that, Bruno Morales?" She planted both hands on her hips and gave him a glare. "Paul is so coming back." Her glance flicked to me. "He would never leave Palo Alto."

"Forgive me." Bruno ran a hand over his head. "I am making a mess of this. It is nothing Paolo has said to me, you understand."

"Just what gave you the idea he was going to bail?" Bridget sounded as indignant as if she had some right to grill Bruno on my behalf. Still speechless, I felt grateful to her.

"I heard from a colleague in Seattle that they want Paolo to interview for some new position they've created that coordinates investigations between different branches." Bruno sighed. "Such a position would be a step up, besides allowing him to stay with his family in this uncertain time. I know nothing of Paolo's feelings in the matter. I shouldn't have said anything."

"Drake wouldn't take that position. He loves his work, his house." Bridget shot me a glance. "His neighbors."

I finally managed to produce my voice. "But his family is in Seattle."

"This is true." Bruno, I could tell, was worried. "And they have all that coffee. Paolo worked so hard to cut down on his coffee consumption. I am afraid that he will come back more addicted than ever."

"If he comes back." That funny sensation in my chest wouldn't go away. It felt like a giant grapefruit spoon had scooped out my heart.

"He'll be back." Bridget spoke up stoutly, and gave me a brief hug. I felt better.

"You are correct, I'm sure." Bruno opened the passenger door of Bridget's car and gestured me in. "Please, forget I said anything. I feel foolish for alluding to something so remote in possibility." He shut the door carefully, and walked away.

Bridget looked at me, her face worried. "He's right,

it's so remote as to be mythical. You know Paul will be back."

"Right." I managed a smile. "I know that."

I asked Bridget about her Christmas shopping process, and she dove into the topic with gusto. It kept her occupied all the way back to my house. And that was a good thing, because I had a hard enough time forcing breath past that empty place in my chest, let alone words.

# 15 _____

**IT** was not quite eight when I got in. Amy was drowsing on the couch, headphones on, book open. The book, I was interested to note, was *The Investor's Guide to the Stock Market*, although she had Bridget's book on the couch next to her. She sat up straighter when I came in, and asked around a yawn, "Is it late? How was your service?"

"It was fine. I was thinking about going over to Drake's place to check the messages and see if he's called. Is that okay?"

"You're getting a lot of mileage out of his house while he's gone, aren't you?" Amy yawned again. "God, I'm so sleepy. I haven't slept this much since I can remember."

"Sleep as much as you want." I turned with one hand on the doorknob. "Will you be okay? Should I hang around?"

"Heck, no, don't stay on my account." She smiled at me and flopped back onto the couch. "I don't want to get in your way. Just pretend I'm not here."

As if I could.

I let myself into Paul's house and looked at the blinking light on his answering machine. I hoped I hadn't missed his call. Then I caught myself. Was this me, getting so hung up on the importance of telephone calls?

I played back the messages on the answering machine, wanting to hear some reassurance from Drake about his future plans, dreading that he might have just left a message saying, the movers are coming, give them the keys. Of course, he wouldn't do that. But having so much emotional dependence on one person was infuriating. I preferred to slip through my life, hindering no one, finding no impediment myself. This policy, though it had served me well for many years, was no longer working. The thought of never seeing Paul again, of living without him, was not just an impediment, it was a total roadblock.

The first message was someone from the city, reminding Drake about a deadline for filing some kind of paperwork. I made a careful note of caller, subject, and phone number in Drake's phone log. The second message was a hang-up. The third was a woman with a cool, authoritative voice and a tone of casual intimacy I found shocking.

"Paul, it's silly to call long-distance to leave you a message, but in case I can't reach you at the hospital, you might pick up your messages from home. Daphne says your dad is better, so I assume we're on for dinner after all. Please give me a call." She didn't give her name or phone number.

I switched off the answering machine. Though I hadn't written anything down, every word of the last message was engraved in my recollection.

My hand holding the pen trembled too much to form letters. I set the pen down on the notebook and found myself standing by the living room window with no thought of how I'd gotten there. Staring blindly into the night, I took deep breaths until the panicky beating of my heart slowed.

It's always painful to face the evidence of your own folly. I had been devastated by a man once before, and it had been life-threatening and horrible and had made me so wary of human contact that I had thought I'd never recover. In the past year, my feelings had changed, due in no small part to Paul Drake. I had resented his pushing and prodding me out of my safely frozen emotions, but I had found myself warming up to relationships with those around me—especially him.

Now that I was thawing nicely, perhaps he'd grown tired of waiting for the rest of the ice to melt.

I leaned my forehead against the cool window glass and tried to control the chaos that swirled through me. Because the living room was dark, I could see clearly through the front window.

Carlotta's car was parked there again. She was actually blocking the end of the driveway, no doubt to see better down it to my cottage in the back.

All those swirling emotions coalesced into one pure feeling: rage. I straightened, my hands tightening into fists. Bad enough that I should have to cope with the fear that I had blown any chance of creating a strong bond with a man I cared for. Bad enough that I had only myself to blame for being so reluctant to, so to speak, go to the mat with Drake. Did I have to be continually hounded for being an outsider, for having no one in my corner, for simply wishing to be left alone?

I headed for the front door, ready to give Carlotta a good reason to fear me.

The phone rang.

I swung around to face it through the archway between

the dining area and living room. It rang again, a shrill, self-important summons that twisted my guts.

Like a somnambulist, I walked toward it. It rang once more. On the fourth ring, the answering machine would pick up. My hand hovered over the receiver. At the last moment, I seized it and brought it to my ear.

"Liz? Are you there?" It was Drake, sounding impatient. "Hello?"

"Drake." My voice was strangled. I cleared my throat. "Hello."

"Are you okay? What's the matter?" The impatience left his voice, replaced by concern.

"Nothing." I had to swallow a couple of times before I could speak. "I hear your dad's better."

"He's a little more comfortable today. They still don't know if the marrow transplant will be needed." He paused. "You must have been talking with Bruno. I'm surprised he picked up my e-mail already."

"You—" I cleared my throat. "You had a message. She said—"

"She?" His voice was sharp.

"The woman who called. She didn't leave a name or time. She said Daphne said your dad was better, so she assumed you could do dinner."

There was silence for a moment. Then Drake spoke. His voice, unexpectedly, was laced with humor. "Are you jealous?"

"Yes." The one word burst from me before I could stop it.

He laughed. "That's good."

"Drake, you can't do this to me."

"I'm sorry, Liz." He spoke more gently. "Suellen's parents and mine are close, and she's Daphne's best

120

friend. We grew up together. Her folks invited my mom and my sister and me for dinner, but we begged off until we knew if we could leave the hospital. See? No big deal." He added thoughtfully, "I don't really know why she called there, though. She knows how to reach us at the hospital."

"Does she know I'm picking up your calls? Have you talked about me?"

The humor left his voice. "I don't discuss our relationship with anyone."

"Because we don't have one?"

"Don't push, Liz."

"She called here to warn me off." I don't know how to play female games, but that doesn't mean I can't recognize them when I see them. "Is she married?"

"You really are jealous, aren't you?"

"Just answer the question."

He sighed. "She was married. It didn't take."

"She cried on your shoulder. She's ready for a family, for a nice little home in the suburbs. She's always thought the two of you would get together sometime. She—"

"Liz, stop." The exasperation was clear. "Sheesh, I was going to put you through the wringer for all the trouble you've gotten into while I was gone. How did you turn the tables on me like this?"

"It's true, isn't it? Her biological clock is ticking—"

"Women must have some kind of weird psychic network link, that's all I can say. You've never even met Suellen."

I took a deep breath and tried for some control. "I'm sorry, Drake. I can't believe I would babble like that. It's just that Bruno said—"

"What did Bruno say? You have been talking to him,

haven't you? Is he making you part of the investigation? I'll have his hide for that."

"Don't be a dork, Paul. He's just doing his job. And speaking of jobs, he said you're being offered a very nice one in Seattle. Where they have all that good coffee, and women who want to embrace domesticity—"

"This is a side of you I hadn't seen before." I couldn't tell what he was thinking from his voice. "I have a very good job in Palo Alto, one that doesn't involve so much paperwork. I have plenty of domesticity there. I have a nice house. I have all the coffee I want. And there's something very important in Palo Alto they don't have here."

"Sunshine? It rains a lot there, I'm told."

"That's true. It rains, and there are no stubborn women who drive incredibly old VW buses and grow divine vegetables."

"And no dogs like Barker. Don't forget him."

"There are certainly no other dogs like Barker anywhere in the world." He was amused again. "What's the boy up to these days? Digging up my yard?"

"He's in ecstasy because of Amy's visit."

"Oh, yes. Amy." Drake smothered a yawn. "What's happening with her? Did she confess to arson?"

"She's pregnant."

A moment of silence. "Whoo. She really knows how to worry her poor old aunt. What are you going to do about it?"

"I don't know. Not my problem."

"Famous last words."

He was right about that. "I hope she goes to Planned Parenthood tomorrow for a checkup and some counseling. It's up to her. She doesn't want to have the baby, but she might change her mind."

"Hey, she could pass it over to you. Instant family."

This careless echo of Bridget's suggestion blew through me like a cold wind. "I hope you're joking, Drake. And it's not funny, anyway."

"No, it's not." He sighed again, the gusty sound whispering into my ear. "What else is happening? Any other dead people cropping up?"

"No, but Carlotta's parked outside again. She's blocking the driveway."

"She's losing her marbles, if she ever had any." Drake was exasperated. "Do me a favor. Don't go confront her. Call the parking enforcement and ask them to send someone out. Don't get involved, Liz."

"It's such a mess." I wondered how tired Drake was of being embroiled in my messes. "I didn't ask for this. It's because people like Carlotta see me as undesirable."

"Don't let them chase you away. Just ignore it, turn it over to the police." His voice was urgent.

"Chase me away, hell! I'm getting mad. What have I done wrong? Nothing! Why should I put up with this?"

"Hmm."

"What does that mean?"

"It means you're showing a lot of spirit for a woman who likes to duck."

"I'm just tired of being pushed around," I muttered.

"I hear you. Just the same, don't go confronting loony old ladies. Just a minute." He put his hand over the receiver; I could hear muffled voices. "I have to go. Remember, I love that you're jealous. But you don't have to worry." He paused. "I miss you like crazy."

"Same here." I controlled the quaver in my voice. "Thanks, Drake. Paul. I—I look forward to your return."

"How much?" His voice was lower, sexier.

"How much?" I ran my tongue over my lips. "Well, I was thinking about becoming more acquainted with your bedroom."

He cleared his throat. "I'll remember that." He spoke to someone else. "Be right there, Daff. Bye, Liz."

I hung up the phone in a completely different frame of mind than I'd answered it. True, this Suellen sounded like the kind of woman who got her way, although how I could tell that from just a seconds-long message was another one of those female mysteries that Drake would decry as impossible. At any rate, he still seemed to prefer an unremarkable-looking ex-vagabond with a gardening jones and an unruly dog. Lucky for me.

I had forgotten to give him his other message, but it didn't matter. Nothing mattered, even Carlotta crouching at the end of my driveway, a self-righteous monitor of my criminal behavior. I drifted into the living room and checked that she was still there, which she was. Putting my hands up against the window to seal light from my eyes, I could even see a little penlight in the front seat with her shadowy bulk crouched behind it. She was reading something, and after our previous encounter, she'd chosen to eschew her dome light. This little precaution only made me smile. Ten minutes ago, I would have been out there, dumping her penlight's batteries on the ground and trying to scare some sense into her.

Just because I was feeling good didn't mean I'd let her completely off the hook. I went back to the kitchen and got out the phone book to chase down the number of the parking enforcers. Before I could open the book, the phone rang again.

I picked it up and caroled a cheery hello, thinking it was Drake with some forgotten tidbit for me.

Bruno's voice. "Good, you are there, Liz. When the line was busy, I hoped you were using the phone. How long have you been there?"

His words alarmed me. "Since Bridget dropped me off. I checked on Amy and then came here to see if Drake had called. He hadn't. But he did, a few minutes after I got here." I glanced toward the front of the house. "Say, Bruno, I was just about to call you folks. Carlotta's been blocking my driveway since before Drake called. Who should I call to have her ticketed? This is really going too far."

"She has been parked?" I heard clacking, and realized Bruno was in note-taking mode.

"What's going on? Are you taking this down?"

"You are a lucky person tonight, Liz. Your Carlotta has been very helpful to you. I will speak with Bridget, and then there will be no problems."

"Why should there be problems?" Apprehensive shivers made their way down my spine. "What are you talking about?"

"Lois Humphries was found at the garden tonight, after you and Bridget left."

The shivering intensified. "Oh, no. No."

"She was dead," Bruno continued, his voice implacable. "She had fallen behind the pile of wood chips the gardeners use for mulching their paths. She was holding a wooden box, about shoe-box size, which we think must contain the husband's ashes she was so careful of. She had not been dead long, Liz. And several people told us that you were there." He paused, but I could say nothing. "You would have made a very convenient scapegoat, if not for your Carlotta. Do not leave

Drake's house. We will be there shortly to interview both of you."

He hung up, and so did I. I tried to take in what he'd said, but it was hard to believe that scrappy little Lois could be dead.

I went back into the living room. Carlotta was still parked out front. Little did she know the effect her spiteful act would have. Nervous giggles bubbled out of me, turning into laughter. I knew it was hysterical, but I let it have its way with me.

It took the sound of cars approaching to sober me. I went to the door to let in Bruno and his minions.

# 16 _____ __

**BRUNO** herded Carlotta into the house, followed closely by Bridget and Officer Rhea. Carlotta sputtered with indignation; Bridget looked worried.

"You do not seem to understand, Mrs. Houseman." Bruno spoke, for him, sternly. "You are blocking a driveway. That is serious. What if emergency vehicles could not get by?"

"I would have moved my car if there had been any need." Carlotta shot me a venomous look.

"I do not understand why you felt this was necessary." Bruno gestured toward Drake's couch. "Please, be comfortable." He nodded at Officer Rhea, who wandered through the archway into the dining area, returning with a chair that she parked in the doorway.

Bridget also sat on the couch. I chose the straight, uncomfortable chair near the hall, the one that's usually piled high with Drake's gym bag and pieces of clothing he's discarded. When I'd tidied it up earlier, I had no idea I'd be sitting there, feeling like a criminal in the witness box.

Bruno sat in the chair by the door, his laptop perched on his knees. He arched his eyebrows at Carlotta, who crossed her arms over her bosom and refused to speak.

"Carlotta has gotten some idea that Liz is dangerous, Bruno." Bridget leaped into the breach. "Why, I don't know." She looked at Carlotta, exasperated. "Her behavior has been totally unacceptable."

"I resent that." Carlotta sat up straighter. "I have only done what needs to be done to protect everyone around here." She stared at me angrily. "You all don't seem to realize the danger you're in. Since this woman somehow managed to snatch poor Vivien's property, people have been murdered. I call that cause and effect."

"Well, I call it libelous. Or is it slanderous?" Bridget's cheeks flamed. "Either way, a lawyer could make a good case against you. And I advise Liz to get one." She turned to Bruno. "I'm glad to see the police are taking this kind of stalking and loose talk seriously. Are you going to arrest her?"

"Arrest me!" Carlotta bridled in outrage. "You must be joking. I've done nothing wrong."

"If spreading lies and rumors isn't wrong, then it wouldn't be wrong for me to do the same to you, is that right?" Bridget's eyes narrowed. "I have a friend at the Forum, as a matter of fact. I think I'll give her this whole story, with a lot of juicy speculation on how you're losing your marbles, Carlotta. Going gaga. Ready for the locked ward."

Bruno cleared his throat, and the two women halted the battle. I had been ready to give Carlotta a piece of my mind, but hadn't been able to get a word in edgewise. Besides, I rather enjoyed hearing Bridget defend me.

"I would like to know what happened after I left you two ladies at your car this evening." Bruno's words fell into the silence. Bridget looked at him speculatively.

"Nothing, as far as I'm concerned," she said. "We

drove home and I dropped Liz off here. She said she was going to check on her niece and then wait in here for a phone call. I went home." She looked at Bruno, and some of the attitude left her voice. "What's happened, Bruno? Why do you need to know this?"

Bruno didn't answer. He turned to Carlotta. "When did you park your car across Liz's driveway, Mrs. Houseman?"

She sniffed. "Not that it's any of your business, but I came directly here after poor Rita's brother spoke so affectingly at the service."

"You weren't here when I dropped off Liz," Bridget said.

"I parked down the street. *She*"—Carlotta pointed at me—"walked off down her driveway, and I realized I couldn't see well enough."

Bruno looked up from his laptop. "What was it you wanted to see, Mrs. Houseman?"

A pregnant pause ensued. Carlotta drew herself up. "I am watching her." She jerked her head toward me. "I should think you would be grateful, Detective Morales. She knows I'm watching. She wouldn't dare do anything for fear of what I'll say." Her eyes glittered.

Bruno was taken aback. "You truly believe Liz to be a murderer, and yet you risk angering her this way?"

"Well, she—I—" Carlotta floundered.

"If she is a killer, why does she not just make you her next victim?" Bruno seemed genuinely interested in the answer.

"That's what I said last night." I finally spoke, but no one paid any attention. They were all watching Carlotta.

Bright spots of red burned on her cheeks. "She wouldn't dare," she said huffily. "She knows I've told everyone about her. If she harmed me, everyone would know."

"So tonight you kept Liz from murdering anyone, is that it?" Bruno clacked away at his computer.

"Bruno!" Bridget sounded incensed. "How could you—"

"Please, Bridget. I am talking to Mrs. Houseman." Bruno fixed Carlotta with a stare. "Is that right? Tonight you saw her go down her driveway? Then you moved your car?"

"Yes." She pressed her lips together, but finally added into the silence, "The kitchen light in this house came on just after I'd parked."

"Did you see Liz in the house?"

"Not really. But it had to be her, gloating over how well she hoodwinked poor Vivien." Carlotta looked around the living room in a disparaging way. "Not that this place is any great shakes, but since she seduced the man she sold it to, I suppose she'll be getting it back."

"That is totally outrageous!" Bridget bounced on the sofa as if she were planning to tackle Carlotta, who shrank back against the cushions.

"Please, Bridget. Allow me to finish. So, Mrs. Houseman, you were parked outside while Liz was in here. She did not leave at any time?"

"She couldn't have driven away, since I was in the way of her getting out of her driveway." Carlotta shot me a triumphant glance. "That's why I parked there."

"And you did not see her leave on foot?"

Carlotta snorted. "That's not likely. She goes everywhere in that wretched old thing she drives. And in fact—"

Bruno looked up from his computer when she faltered. "What, Mrs. Houseman?"

"I saw a little movement back in the kitchen. I don't

think she'd realized I was here." Carlotta wouldn't look at me. She spoke as if I wasn't even in the room. "I mean, she didn't come out and yell at me like she did last night. I suppose she will try to murder me one of these days, and it will be your fault for not locking her up where she belongs."

"Bruno, what is it?" Bridget had realized something was going on. She looked at me anxiously.

"There has been another death."

"Aha!" Carlotta was triumphant. "I knew it!"

"The death occurred after the meeting at the garden. During that time, I observed Liz until she left with Bridget. Then you began your surveillance of her." Bruno looked at Carlotta and allowed himself to smile. "Thanks to you, Ms. Sullivan has a cast-iron alibi."

"Who was killed?" Bridget twisted her hands together. "This is terrible!"

Bruno watched Carlotta, who had lost the power of speech, if her gaping jaw was any indicator. "Lois Humphries. We have not yet decided how she died. It is possible she simply had a heart attack."

"Lois?" Carlotta rose to her feet. "Lois is dead?" She stared at Bruno, then around the room. "She—but this can't be. She said—"

"What did she say, Mrs. Houseman? When did you speak with her?"

"I saw her," Carlotta whispered dazedly. "I saw her at the garden tonight. She was so angry when they wanted to set up a place for the flowers and candles in front of her plot. She made them move it outside by the fence. And she said—"

Her jaw worked. Bruno waited patiently. Bridget

opened her mouth, then closed it again at Bruno's commanding glance. Officer Rhea shifted in her chair, and the implements on her belt clanked faintly.

"She said she would pay back the person who'd desecrated her garden," Carlotta continued, her voice faint. "I thought she meant Liz."

"So you parked here, hoping to see a fight?" Bridget bounced on the sofa again. "I've never heard anything so outrageous in my life! You ought to be ashamed!"

Carlotta didn't hear her. She looked as if she might faint. Officer Rhea went into the kitchen and ran a glass of water, but Carlotta didn't even see her offer it. "I thought she was coming over here tonight to have it out with Liz." She lifted dazed eyes to Bruno. "If it wasn't Liz, then who was it?"

"That," said Bruno, making a final note on his computer, "is what we would all like to know."

# 17 _____

I sat in the waiting room at the Planned Parenthood clinic, trying to read an out-of-date *People* magazine. Amy was seeing the doctor for a pregnancy test and presentation of her options. She had called first thing that morning to find out if it was legal for her to get an abortion in California without her parents' knowledge or permission. It was.

"It will cost over three hundred dollars." Amy had been more shocked by that than by anything else. "Unless I have MediCal, whatever that is."

"You don't. It's for California residents."

"I hate Colorado," Amy burst out. "I don't want to go back."

That, too, was troubling.

Amy hadn't asked me for any money, which was fortunate. Not that I wouldn't have dipped into my precious little savings on her behalf, but the insecurities of my life are such that I hoard every dime against an uncertain future. Aside from that, it seemed to me that it was up to Amy to pay for what she wanted so badly. I was still too ambivalent about the whole thing to be comfortable footing the bill.

I stared at the glossy faces in the magazine on my lap,

but the coy snippets of gossip meant less than nothing to me—I had never heard of the TV stars, since I don't have a TV, and the only movies I saw were those rented by Drake on occasion, which tended toward art films and classics. He'd taken me to a first-run movie once, but the cost was so incredible I felt guilty all the way through. Perhaps he's right when he says I've been ruined for normal life.

Instead of the beautiful faces on the page, I kept seeing Lois Humphries—self-righteous, thin-lipped, disapproving, but still a person who worked hard for what she believed in. Now she was dead, and perhaps because of her hard work. I couldn't help but wonder if her death happened through something at the garden. It seemed unlikely that two accidental deaths could occur so close together. One, or both, must have been caused by human machinations. But why would Lois be killed?

Unless she knew something about Rita's death. Something that someone else had wanted to keep concealed.

I remembered her visit to me—was it only two days ago? Her perturbation, her anxiety once it was clear to her that I had nothing to hide. She had known something, and she had chosen to deal with it herself instead of telling the police.

The baby next to me began wailing, jolting me from my thoughts. The girl in charge of the baby was very young, her shoulders bowed as if she carried the troubles of the universe instead of one small baby. She should have been strolling through the mall with her friends, giggling and stopping at the food court. Instead, she *was* the food court, trying to give her baby a bottle while rummaging in the enormous bag of stuff with her other hand.

"Can I help?" I indicated the bag. "What are you looking for? Perhaps I can get it for you."

"*Gracias.*" Looking frightened, she tightened her grip on the baby. "I need nothing, thank you."

She abandoned her attempt to find whatever it was in the bag, and the infant quieted when she directed all her attention toward giving it the bottle. I wondered why she didn't breast-feed, why she was alone when she couldn't have been more than fifteen, whether the father of her baby spent any time with her and it. But I couldn't ask.

The outer door opened and a vivacious brunette swept in, her V-necked green scrubs proclaiming her a health-care professional. She carried a paper bag, and she stopped at the reception desk to pull out a tall, capped cup and hand it over to the woman behind the desk, who took it thankfully.

The brunette lingered, uncapping her own cup. "He's out there again," she said ominously.

The woman behind the reception desk looked alarmed. "Oh, no."

"Yes." The brunette shook her head. "I told him he had to get back, that he wasn't allowed to stand so close. But he didn't pay much attention. You may have to call the cops."

The woman behind the desk seemed resigned. "I'll get Evelyn to come over and escort people first," she said, pulling the phone toward her.

A nurse came into the waiting room. She took a clipboard from a rack of them by the door and announced, "Teresa Hidalgo."

The girl next to me stood up, clutching her baby, the enormous bag bulging off her shoulder. "This way," the nurse said, and Teresa disappeared.

I went back to my magazine, but the people in it

seemed even further from real life. They were in love, engaged, in counseling, divorcing, seeing someone new. What did it matter?

Amy returned, followed by a slight young woman in a white coat, with a dark, glowing complexion and short dreadlocks springing from a wide forehead. "Hello," she said, offering a firm handshake when I joined Amy. "I'm Dr. Jones. Amy's doing fine, and I've given her a bunch of stuff to read." She turned to Amy, who clutched her pile of literature with a dazed expression. "You should go ahead and make an appointment now, and if you decide against the procedure, you can cancel it. But you should decide soon."

Amy tightened her grip on the literature. "Okay," she mumbled. "Thanks, Dr. Jones."

She went to make her appointment at the desk, and Dr. Jones smiled at me. "Amy seems very sensible, very centered."

"Yes, I think she is." Through the consulting room door, I could see Teresa Hidalgo being weighed while the nurse held her baby. "Do you all take care of babies here, too?"

"No." Dr. Jones glanced over her shoulder. "We do offer gynecological care and contraceptives, though. The moms-to-be come to us throughout their pregnancies, and after the birth, too. If Amy chooses to have her baby, we'll be happy to provide her prenatal checkups. Then she'd deliver at Stanford."

This was another stunning thought. "But—she doesn't live here. I mean, she's from Denver."

Dr. Jones wrinkled her forehead. "Somehow I got the idea—well, Amy will talk about it with you, I'm sure."

Her brown eyes were sympathetic, her rich voice soft. "I understand your family is Catholic."

"Yes, very. She hasn't told them about her—condition. They'd hit the roof."

"What do you think about that?"

"She's making her own decisions. What I think doesn't matter."

"Well, that's not really true. But it's good you're standing by." Dr. Jones gave me a pat and went back to the consulting rooms.

While Amy waited at the appointment desk, I drifted over to the clinic's door and looked through. A man stood at the sidewalk, his back to the clinic, holding up a large sign toward the traffic on Middlefield. Something about him was familiar. I assumed he was an antiabortion protester, and I didn't think I knew any men foolhardy enough to tell women how to use their bodies.

The man wore a billed hat pulled low over his eyes and a fleecy vest with the collar up around his ears, despite the mildness of the November day. While I watched, a pair of women approached the clinic, the younger one moving slowly, her older companion supporting her. The older woman—her mother?—took one horrified look at the sign the man carried and averted her eyes. The man gestured with his sign, and the younger woman shrank away, hesitating.

I barged out the door, but the older woman was already coping with the problem. "Please move aside, sir," she said with gentle dignity. "My daughter has had a miscarriage and needs to see her doctor."

I tapped the man on the shoulder. "Excuse me."

The woman hustled her daughter past as the man turned to face me. It was Tom Dancey.

"Mr. Dancey. What a surprise to see you here."

He pulled the hat lower over his eyes. "Do I know you?"

"I'm one of the community gardeners. You gave a very affecting speech at the garden last night." I looked at the sign he carried and nearly threw up. Under a huge, stomach-wrenching, color picture of mangled tissue and blood, large red letters asked ARE YOU A MURDERER? It was no wonder the young woman had hesitated to pass by.

"That's really nasty." I noticed that cars on Middlefield Road were slowing down to read the sign, maybe hoping we were going to have a Confrontation with a capital *C*. "Why are you doing this, Mr. Dancey? I mean, the women who come here face hard enough choices."

His face was stony, his gaze turned away. "What happens in there is murder, plain and simple. Are you here to murder a baby?" He glanced at me briefly, then turned away, his sign facing toward Middlefield Road.

"I don't think you have a clue what happens inside." I wanted to shake him, but contented myself with moving around to face him. "The woman you just harassed had a miscarriage. Does that sound like abortion? Maybe she wanted that baby desperately and having to pass your sign is just more torture. I sat next to a girl—not even sixteen. She had a tiny baby that will take over her life for the next twenty years. I didn't see the father there."

He shook his head as if shaking off my words. I stepped closer, impelled out of my usual observer status by some emotion I couldn't quantify. "Tell me, Mr. Dancey. Tom. If you want to have a positive effect on this problem, why aren't you over at the middle school, at the high school, asking the fathers of those babies what they were thinking of? Why are you bothering these women?"

He didn't even look at me. "You have your views, I have mine. Freedom of speech guarantees me a hearing."

"I call this harassment, not freedom of speech. You're picking out the most vulnerable segment of society and persecuting—"

Stung, he raised his voice. "I'll tell you who's vulnerable. Those babies! What about them?" He shook his sign at me. "What gives a woman the right to flush my baby away?"

Amy came out of the clinic. I didn't want her to see Tom Dancey's horrible picture, but by arguing with him, I had made sure to draw her attention to it. I made a vain attempt to block her view. "Don't look, honey."

She looked anyway, and quickly averted her eyes.

Tom Dancey regarded her sadly. "So, young woman. Are you going to murder a baby?" He shook his head. "Death everywhere. Everyone dies. Are you ready to die?"

The hairs stood up on the back of my neck. Amy shrank away. I wanted to hurry her to the car, but I had to lay to rest the horrid suspicion that leaped into my head.

"Why do you say that, Tom?" I spoke in my gentlest tone of voice, gesturing to Amy behind my back to go wait for me in Babe. "Did you know that someone else died at the garden last night?"

Behind me, I could hear Amy's gasp. So much for keeping her out of it. I should never have started my inquisition, but having begun, I couldn't leave until I had some answers.

Tom stared at me blankly. "Someone else dead?" He frowned. "Rita died there. At the garden."

"I know."

"She said it was nothing to do with me." His eyes were

139

earnest, fixed on mine. "But I told her that was wrong. I told her—"

"What? What did you tell her?"

He shook his head again, quickly, as if to clear away some foreign influence. When he looked at me again, his gaze was shuttered. "Who did you say you were?"

"One of the gardeners." I hesitated. "Look, Tom. Mr. Dancey. It sounds like you know something the police should know. If Rita told you anything—if you have any idea of who might have wished to harm her—"

"What are you talking about? Her death was an accident!" He waved his sign in agitation. "That's what the officer told me. An accident—she tripped over a rake or something. Are you suggesting that she was—"

"Murdered." I glanced at his sign. "There is some question about that, I believe. Look, give Bruno Morales a call—he's the detective in charge."

"I had a message from him on the office phone this morning." Tom Dancey looked bewildered. "But—I had to come here. Now that Rita's gone—I had to let people know." Suddenly he lunged past me and grabbed Amy's arm. She pulled away, but he tightened his grip. "If she hadn't killed my baby," he said urgently, "I'd have something now. Something of ours. Don't do it. Don't kill—"

"Now, Tom." An authoritative female voice spoke up. "You know you promised not to confront or harass our clients." The woman who spoke was stout, middle-aged, well-groomed. She walked up to Tom Dancey and pried his hands away from Amy. "You just go on, dear. He won't hurt you."

Amy scuttled a few feet. "Aunt Liz," she said, her voice imploring.

"I'm coming." I turned back to Tom Dancey, but he was already walking away, his sign down, his head lowered, too.

"Sorry about that," the woman said. "He sometimes gets emotional. But he's generally pretty good about leaving the younger girls alone."

"Is he here often?" I watched him turn the corner, the sign dragging behind him as if he'd forgotten it and its horrid message.

"He was here every day for a few months about a year ago. That's when we got the restraining order. Lately, he hasn't been around. I was surprised to get a call about him today." She looked speculative. "Something must have set him off."

"He seemed a bit unbalanced."

She sighed. "He's really a very nice man. I actually know his family. He's as sane as can be most of the time, but—" She shut her lips firmly, and I knew there'd be no more confidences from her.

"Thanks for your help," I said, and went to join Amy in the parking lot.

She was on me the minute I got into Babe. "Who was that man? What did he mean? And what was that about murders at the garden?"

"His stepsister died Saturday at the community garden—maybe an accident."

"It didn't sound like he thought of her as a sister," Amy said shrewdly. "Sounds like he got her pregnant and she had an abortion."

"It sounded like that to me, too."

"And now she's dead. Is he over the edge? Did you say someone else died last night?"

"Another woman—a garden volunteer. Heart attack, Bruno thinks."

"People die from having babies, too." Amy's voice was low. "Dr. Jones told me the risks. It sounds scary. Embolisms, hemorrhages—"

"Women do have babies safely, too, though. Look around you. Plenty of old mothers still alive and kicking."

"I am going to have an abortion." Amy's voice was quiet but firm. "I made the appointment. I want this all over with."

"It's up to you." I felt an odd mixture of relief and regret. Certainly all our lives would be easier if Amy went ahead with her plans. Renee, I thought, had tacitly given her permission by not forcing the issue, and she would no doubt be relieved as well that her only daughter wasn't bringing disgrace on the name of Sullivan. And certainly, no matter what anyone said, I didn't want to get mixed up in imminent babyhood. But it was impossible not to feel regret no matter what choice Amy made. In this case, the regret was for the waste of life. It is wasted every day, everywhere, by women and especially by men, by the old as well as the young, by those who do not kill but simply do not or cannot live fully. But the universal nature of such waste doesn't mean that we shouldn't mourn its passing.

"It's spooky," Amy said, getting away from her own predicament. "That people died at the garden, of all places. Aren't you scared to go there?"

"Not at all. Not during the day, anyway. That's where we're going as soon as we pick up our tools and I get my overalls, in fact."

"Oh." Amy shivered. "I never thought there'd be so

many deaths in a place like this." She gestured at the nice bungalows and tidy lawns we drove past on our way home.

"People who live here are surprised, too. Some of them think it's me."

"They think you're killing people?" Amy was horrified. "Aunt Liz!"

"Not so much that." I didn't think even Carlotta really believed I was killing people. "Just that undesirable elements like me precipitate violence."

"That is so lame. They can't say stuff like that about you!"

"It's nothing. The people whose opinions matter to me won't listen to the gossip, and I don't care about the others."

This piece of philosophy was not well received by Amy. "That's just bullshit, Aunt Liz. This girl in school, some other girls didn't like her and started this whispering thing, and she was all, like, 'I don't care if they say I'm a slut, I know I'm not and so do my friends.' But it was awful for her, and there were fights in gym class, and the whole school knew, and finally she transferred."

"That sounds pretty gruesome. Are you afraid they'll do something like that to you?"

Amy shook her head. "I'm, like, not popular enough," she said simply. "And no one will know anything about it, because the problem will be over when I get back."

We were both silent for a while, and then Amy roused herself. "So are we digging at the garden today? Or what?"

"I don't know. Bridget will be there—"

"Great." Amy brightened. "Mrs. Montrose is very kind, isn't she? I got the feeling she didn't want me to have an abortion, but she wouldn't say anything about it. And it was nice of her to lend me that book. I found out some stuff. But it's just so gross—really, Aunt Liz, you can't think. I mean, I don't know how anyone can stand to breast-feed. Milk coming out of you—yuck. And pictures of babies being born—how can anyone live through that?"

"They have been, for the most part, since the human race began."

"Well, I think it's unfair." Amy began to wax indignant. "Why should it be up to women? Men have the fun, too, and then women have to go through all that blood and pain and stuff. And don't give me that biblical thing. If I truly thought God wanted to punish Eve for being smarter than Adam, I'd have to, you know, reexamine everything in my life and all."

"But you're still a Catholic? How can you reconcile that with what you're going to do?" As soon as I asked the question, I was sorry.

She didn't answer for a moment, then her voice was low. "I don't know, Aunt Liz. I mean, I love the church. I love the ritual. Did you know I wanted to be a nun for a while when I was ten? But now—I look at it and all I see is a bunch of old men telling me what to do. How do they know what's the best thing? Just because something's been written down for thousands of years, does that make it still right?" She sighed. "I haven't been able to go to confession for a while. And if I do this abortion—will they excommunicate me?"

"I don't think so." I didn't want to say anything else. Since abandoning my natal religion, I have spent years slowly formulating my own belief system, which is so personal that it could have no meaning for anyone but me.

I parked in the driveway, and Amy touched my arm. "I'm glad I'm with you, Aunt Liz." She smiled at me, her eyes full of trust. "I know you'll stand by."

"Yes. I will do that, Amy."

## 18

WE went inside, since I wanted to get my garden overalls. One of my compulsive habits of thrift is to do as little laundry as possible. When I lived in the bus, my wardrobe was minimal—something like those three simple pieces that Nordstrom touts in their ad, but far lower on the fashion scale. I didn't do temp work then, and I could wear every stitch I owned in four days, necessitating frequent trips to the laundromat.

Now I had my own washer, but I was as stingy with it as any old miser. I had amassed a stock of aprons, which unfashionable garment I wore in the kitchen to keep off gratuitous splashes of food. And I had a fine pair of overalls for the garden. They were roomy enough to go over regular clothes, if all I had time for was some quick weeding. I hung them in the back porch and washed them only when they had been consorting with something smelly.

While Amy foraged in the refrigerator, I put on my overalls and my work shoes—a pair of old wellies I'd found at a garage sale. The tops had been sun-damaged and had torn out at the sides where a previous owner had grasped them for pulling on. But when I cut off the tops with my utility knife, I had a pair of waterproof shoes that did the job as well as any in the upscale garden shops.

Together Amy and I put the shovel and rake and various buckets in the car. Amy sniffed suspiciously at one lidded bucket. "This isn't chicken manure, is it?"

"No. I remember how you didn't like the chicken manure experience."

She sniffed again. "This has a very similar stink."

"It's rabbit manure. Supposed to be very mellow and smell-free. And I've been composting it for a while." I took the bucket from her and put it in the back of Babe. "Have we got everything?"

"We've got a lot, for sure." Amy's mood was not bettered by the bucket of rabbit poop. She dusted off her hands ostentatiously and reached into her pocket to extract a paper towel–wrapped bundle. Inside were stacks of crackers and some of the presliced cheese she liked, folded into quarters. She offered me one of the stacks, but I declined.

"So you're going to want me to dig that junk in at the garden, aren't you?" Amy spoke through a mouthful of cracker.

"Yes, I'm going to try planting potatoes early and gamble that we'll have a mild winter and they won't freeze." Turning onto Middlefield, I ran through a mental checklist of the equipment we'd loaded. "Dang! I forgot the potatoes."

"We can go back and get them."

"No, I told Bruno we'd be there at eleven."

"Bruno? Mr. Morales?" Amy stopped chewing to stare at me. "Are the police going to be there?"

"It's no big deal. He wants Bridget and me to go around the garden with him and tell him whose plots are

147

whose. I don't really know all that many, but he's probably got other people doing the same thing for him."

"Well, maybe I shouldn't come." She looked at me, worried. "Maybe he won't want me in the way."

"You won't be in the way. You'll just be digging." I glanced at her. "If you think it's okay in your condition."

"I'm not sick or anything. Exercise is good for me." Amy didn't look at me. She watched the houses go by out the window. "It's funny how I stopped feeling sick and everything after I got here."

"A whole day ago."

"Well, even before, really. Except for the airplane, my stomach hasn't bothered me for a few days." She scowled. "But my guts still feel so weird. Like really heavy-duty PMS, you know?"

I knew, because I'd been pregnant once for a very little while. I hadn't been driven to the extreme Amy was thinking about, though. My pregnancy had ended of its own accord, with a little help from my then-husband. And I wasn't sorry that getting pregnant again was no longer an option in my life. I was just sorry that Amy had to do her learning on the subject the hard way.

She seemed relatively cheerful, however, maybe because she'd made a decision and taken steps. At the garden, she carried in the bucket of rabbit manure without protest. I had time to spread it over the patch I wanted dug, and to top it off with the bucket of home-made compost, before Bruno showed up. Bridget came through the gate a few minutes later, rushing from her preschool commitment.

Bridget greeted Amy warmly. I could see she wanted to ask how it had gone at the doctor's that morning, but Bruno was in a hurry. He pulled out his laptop and herded us over to the path, leaving Amy shoveling in my plot.

"Do either of you mind if I tape this conversation?" Bruno reached into his breast pocket and showed us a tiny tape recorder, already going. "I will be putting the pertinent things directly into the computer. But the tape is useful in case I miss something the first time. If anything on the tape is necessary to enter as evidence, you will be asked to sign a typed transcription. You are at liberty not to answer any question if you do not wish to."

"This sounds serious." Bridget watched as Bruno put the little tape recorder back in his pocket. "I don't know how we can help you."

He pulled one of my empty plastic buckets into the path, turned it over, and sat on it. Amy slowed her digging, her head cocked, but with his back to her, Bruno must have been barely audible. He opened the laptop and set it on his knees. "You have used a plot at the community garden for how long?" Bruno looked at me, then Bridget. I answered first.

"More than three years."

"I've been here for a couple of years," Bridget said. "I was at the downtown one before."

"Have you had the same neighboring gardeners the whole time?"

I shook my head, and Bridget nodded. "New people next to me," I told him. "But some people have the same plot for many years. Tamiko's been across the way since I've been here. And Webster Powell, next to her. And Lois around the corner there."

"That is Tamiko's plot?" Bruno glanced across the path, then turned to look at Amy. "Let us go over and look at it more closely."

I had spread the rabbit poop on the back part of my plot, so by the time we reached the border between Tamiko and Webster we were out of Amy's earshot. Tamiko had a compost pile in her front corner, by the path; Webster's elegant plastic composter was in his back corner, by the outside fence.

I remembered my first day at the garden, when I'd known no one. The plot I'd been assigned had been neglected for a season, and I cleared weeds and dead tomato vines for a couple of hours. Tamiko had introduced herself, asked me to let her know if the sunflowers she'd planted began to shade my garden as they grew, and offered me an extra cucumber seedling. She wasn't chatty, but she always found time to admire something in my garden.

I expected Bruno to ask about Tamiko's personal life, about which I knew nothing at all. Instead he said, "What kind of gardener is she?"

It took me off guard. Bridget was the first to answer. "Hmm. Well, she's very neat. No weeds, no Bermuda grass. She grows a lot of flowers and herbs and some exotic-looking Japanese veggies. She's always handing out sprigs of stuff." Bridget looked at me.

"She has good equipment, but not that shiny kind of yuppie garden gear. Everything well-used."

Bruno mulled over Tamiko's tidy plot. "Did she ever express resentment at Ms. Dancey's activities?"

"Not to me," I said.

Bridget spoke up. "Tamiko isn't much to gossip or complain about people behind their backs."

"Has she ever mentioned Ms. Dancey to either of you in any context?"

I told him the incident I'd mentioned to Tamiko the

previous night. "Once Tamiko asked if I'd gotten the latest garden letter, which was about raspberry canes. We're not supposed to plant them anymore, or anything invasive. She said Rita should make Webster tear out those raspberries. He'd just planted them, so it would have been easy, then." I pointed at the flourishing canes. "Not so easy now. Anyway, Tamiko said Rita wouldn't take it up with Webster because they were dating, and he wouldn't listen to anyone else. But last night she said she didn't remember it at all."

Bruno perched the laptop on the edge of Tamiko's compost bin and clacked away. I wondered what the sound of computer keys did to his tape recorder. "So this next one is Webster Powell's garden?"

"Yeah," Bridget said. "He keeps it very tidy, I'll give him that. But he's not cooperative. Tamiko told him about the raspberries, but he just wouldn't listen. She has to dig out suckers constantly. But he gets very bent if someone else breaks a rule that affects him." Bridget warmed to her theme. "Do you know, he accused Liz of throwing Bermuda grass into his garden. Can you imagine? As if Liz could be so spiteful."

"Right." Bruno looked bemused. "Bermuda grass could certainly cause hostility between gardeners. It is very hard to get rid of."

"Some people," Bridget said darkly, "have resorted to forbidden chemicals to control it. Rumor has it that Lois and maybe Webster sprayed Roundup outside the fence by their gardens, and on the paths, too. Supposedly Rita looked the other way, maybe even used it herself."

Bruno took his cue from the horror in Bridget's voice. "That is very bad, right?"

"It's not as bad as some herbicides, but it's pretty

151

bad." Bridget looked to me for confirmation. "Right, Liz?"

"It does get rid of the Bermuda grass, but it can drift onto other people's gardens and kill stuff." I hesitated, and added, "But the people next to the fence really have trouble getting rid of the noxious weed. You can see why they use Roundup, even though it's forbidden."

"So did many people dislike Rita for allowing this to go on?" Bruno held his pen poised over his notebook.

I looked at him. "You know, Bruno, we were all hoping that these deaths were accidental. Sounds like you have other ideas."

Bruno looked unhappy. He chose his words carefully. "One or both of them could be an accident. But I do not think so. This"—he tapped his chest, presumably his heart or intuition—"tells me someone meant Rita to die. And if someone meant that, it is more than likely Lois, too, was murdered."

A cold wind had blown clouds over the sun, making the garden seem vast and dark. Dead leaves sifted out of the encircling plum trees, fluttering to the ground in a constant susurration.

Bruno looked over Webster's plot. "Tell me something about Mr. Powell's gardening style."

"Well," Bridget began, "Webster is kind of an obsessive person. He's done some consulting work for Emery, so I know a bit about him. Everything has to be just so. He carries that over to his gardening, I guess." She glanced at me, and I nodded.

"A couple of months ago he claimed someone had come into his garden and touched his compost bin. The gloves he'd left on top had been knocked off. I mean, who knows how they leave their garden gloves?"

"He shouldn't leave them anyway," Bridget added. "I never leave anything here. Stuff gets stolen."

"That's true," I said. "I got this rusty old wheelbarrow at a garage sale, thinking no one would bother stealing it. I was wrong."

Bruno looked shocked. "The gardeners steal from one another?"

"It's not necessarily the gardeners," Bridget said. "A lot of people walk through every day who don't garden here. They help themselves to anything growing near the path—especially berries. People seem to think it's just free groceries. Maybe they feel the same about tools and such. Or maybe it's some gardener in a hurry who borrows something without asking and forgets to put it back."

I pointed out Webster's compost bin back by the fence. "That's a really bad place to leave anything you value. Anyone using the path could have just reached over the fence and taken the gloves. Probably they were trying to do just that and dropped them."

"Webster especially needs to be careful," Bridget sniffed, "because he's got every fancy tool they sell at Smith and Hawken. Those were probably very nice gloves."

"You don't like him." At least Bruno didn't write that observation down.

"He's one of those people who grub around in the dirt and never look dirty," Bridget admitted sheepishly. "That's really what I hold against him."

"I hardly know him." I tried to leave it at that, but Bruno's raised eyebrows compelled me to add, "He shouldn't have been so ready to believe badly of me. That kinda soured me on him."

"He dated one of the programmers in Emery's company for a while." Bridget's sense of fairness came to the fore. "She seemed to think he was okay."

"He works for Emery, you said?" Bruno made another note.

"I heard he's really, really good at what he does and gets paid really well for it."

"Perhaps I will talk to Emery." Bruno added a note or two and closed his computer. "Now, let us go look at Lois Humphries's plot."

I moved restlessly. "Haven't you already combed it pretty well?"

Bruno led the way down the path toward Lois's plot, still brightly festooned with caution tape. Additional tape fluttered outside the fence, on the other side of the perimeter path. The heap of wood chips, periodically dumped by city maintenance workers near the perimeter path for gardeners to use as mulch, was cordoned off. My stomach clenched.

Bridget stopped, looking at the pile of wood chips. "Is that where she was found?"

"Yes." Bruno stopped, too. "Behind, under those bushes. She held very tightly to a wooden box, which we believe holds the ashes of her husband. Our preliminary investigation has not found a cause of death."

"I thought she had a heart attack," Bridget said.

Bruno's expression hardened. "It's true she had recently been diagnosed with angina, according to her family doctor. He said she was in denial—would overdo, get chest pains, get frightened and pull back. Then she'd feel fine and overdo again. Such a person may have a fatal attack that is caused by outside forces." He looked at us sharply. "Were you unaware of her heart condition?"

"I knew nothing about it. She was always bustling

154

around digging and hauling bags of stuff." Bridget looked at me.

"Someone ragged her a little the other morning for not digging, and she said it was her heart. But frankly, I got the idea that was just an excuse." We had come to Lois's garden plot by then, and I pointed to the trench. "After all, she was double-digging her garden, even though it didn't really need it. No one would undertake that without feeling pretty healthy."

Bruno opened the laptop and wrote some more. "Who else was there when Lois mentioned her heart?"

"I don't really remember. A couple of people I didn't know, and Rita. In fact, Rita was the one who suggested that Lois dig her own holes." I couldn't summon up any clearer picture. "Sorry, Bruno. I know there were several folks around. Just don't remember them."

Bridget glanced at her watch. "How much longer will this take? I've got a lot to do this morning."

I looked through the clutter of trellises and cornstalks that intervened between my plot and Lois's. Amy's red T-shirt made a bright spot in the dun-colored foliage. "Yeah, I've got to go supervise my helper or she might dig up all my seedlings."

"You are both doing very well at giving me your observations. I will not keep you much longer." Bruno looked up from his laptop. "What kind of gardener was Lois?"

"She was the one who rounded up people to volunteer for stuff like path maintenance," Bridget said. "She's been—she had been here since the garden started, and she knew everything and everyone."

"She and her husband were here every day," I added. "Even when he couldn't work anymore, he'd come and

155

sit on that chair while she did the work." I nodded toward the plastic lawn chair in a corner of Lois's garden, next to a platform where the wooden chest holding his ashes had stood. "I'm pretty sure she wasn't broadcasting her heart problem. You could ask my near–Siamese twin, Carlotta, about that. She'd know, if anyone did."

"So, was Lois a very good gardener?"

"She was—strict. Had her veggies under stern control. First sign of mildew or blight, they were outta there."

"She didn't cut any slack," Bridget agreed. "Not for plants or people."

Bruno typed some more. After a few more questions, he let us go. Bridget bustled off, and I turned toward my plot, to help Amy finish shaping the beds. But Bridget's final remark about Lois echoed in my brain. Lois hadn't wanted to cut me any slack, but she'd changed her mind.

Was there someone else she didn't approve of, someone else breaking rules she thought were inviolable? What would have happened if she'd tried to uproot someone from the garden who didn't want to go?

And why would anyone murder to keep from being thrown out of the garden? It didn't make any sense.

# 19

AMY met me with mutiny, her hands on her hips, her mouth set stubbornly. "I'm not shoveling any more shit today," she said, narrowing her eyes at me. "This is too totally gross for anyone, even if they weren't pregnant and about to hurl at any minute."

"I'm sorry." I hurried forward and took the shovel from her hand. "You have to admit it's not nearly as bad as chicken manure. I guess I didn't compost it enough."

She had done most of the area I'd spread, and I turned under the rest of it. After I raked in more compost, Amy felt better. We harvested some of the small golden beets and cut a lot of spinach and lettuce.

Webster appeared while we were harvesting, carrying his tools in from the parking lot. I glanced up when he went by, but he walked briskly on without looking around. He used a fancy oscillating hoe on one of his beautifully mounded beds, shaving off weed seedlings just below the surface of the dirt. It was very efficient. I wondered for a moment what it would be like to have a variety of special tools, instead of my garage sale trio of hoe, rake, and shovel.

I went back to clipping lettuce, but a little later a shadow fell over the bed, and when I looked up, Webster was standing there. He seemed a little uncertain. One hand was behind his back.

"Um, Liz—"

"Hi, Webster." It was a good thing, I decided, that Webster hadn't been around half an hour earlier to see Bruno checking out his plot.

He brought his hand around from behind his back. It held a small cardboard box with several fava bean sprouts sticking up from it. "I had to thin in a couple of places. I was just going to toss these into the compost, but I wondered if you'd want them."

"Thanks." I took the box, touched. Webster's nose wrinkled as the breeze brought him a hint of what we'd been digging.

"No problem. Hope they work for you." He waved and went back to pick up his tools. Then he left the garden, back through the trees to the parking lot.

Amy started watering, and I followed her with a bag of wheat bran. I was sprinkling it around the lettuce to make a snail barrier, when a man spoke from the path behind me.

"Excuse me." The deep voice sounded familiar. "You're here. I just thought—I really didn't think, I guess—"

I looked around. Tom Dancey stood in the path. He still wore the vest and baseball cap, but this time the cap was pushed back. I could see his eyes, hesitant and defiant at the same time.

"Mr. Dancey." I glanced over my shoulder at Amy. Her back was turned; she hadn't heard us over the noise of the water. "What are you doing here? I warn you, if you try to upset my niece again—"

"I won't," he said swiftly, holding up a hand to stop my furious whisper. "I—this is about something totally different. You said—you mentioned my . . . sister, Rita. I wanted—"

"How did you find me? Have you been following me?"

"No, no." He didn't look dangerous. In fact, he looked abashed, backing off a step. "I was thinking. About Rita. I've just been . . . driving around. Thinking about Rita. So I thought I'd come here and see—I never dreamed you'd actually be here. I just thought maybe someone would, someone who could tell me—"

"Tell you what? You should be asking the police about this. Bruno Morales—"

"I know, I know. I'm going to get in touch with him. But I just wanted to know—need to know." His voice sounded urgent. "Who, Ms.—um? Who would want to hurt Rita?"

"Mr. Dancey, they don't know that anyone wanted to hurt her."

"But someone did." He nodded his head at me. His face was strongly shaped, with a look of intelligence, but his manner seemed demented, in a low-key way. "Yes. Someone hurt her. Someone had a hand in killing her. I'm almost sure of it. And it had to be one of these gardeners. Or maybe a rapist, coming along—"

"In the middle of the morning, with people all around? It doesn't sound like a rapist, and she wasn't molested."

He shook his head, back and forth, as he had earlier at Planned Parenthood. "No. No. I know that. But did you know—did you see—?" He put out one hand. "Say, what is your name, anyway? I'm Tom Dancey, as you know." He made the introduction very naturally, producing a smile of great charm.

"Mr. Dancey." It was Amy's clear voice, coming from

behind my shoulder. "I think you need to see a therapist or something. You're acting totally spaced and weird, you know that?" She sounded indignant.

Tom Dancey gaped at her. "Miss—I'm sorry."

"Sorry doesn't cut it. You're not in good shape. Why don't you get yourself together before you go telling other people what to do?"

"Amy—"

She overrode my attempt to shut her down. "You know, some girl might just take you seriously some time. And she might just have a baby because of your ugly pictures. And she might just bring that baby to you, because you shoved yourself into her life and influenced the decision she made. And you might just find yourself stuck with some tiny, little baby to take care of for the rest of your life. You have to find child care, you have to feed it, you have to jump when it cries. Then maybe you'd have a better understanding than you do!"

Tom Dancey hadn't tried to interrupt this tirade. He stood with his head bowed, hands shoved into the pockets of his fleece vest. But when Amy finally finished, he shot her a glance. "I'm sorry, Miss. I—happen to have very strong beliefs. But I didn't come here to talk about—abortion." He turned to me. "I want to ask you some things about Rita. I have to know."

"Don't talk to him, Aunt Liz," Amy commanded, her face still flushed. "Don't give him the slightest speck of information."

"Excuse me for a minute," I said to Dancey. Then I took Amy's arm and urged her to the back of the garden.

"Amy, obviously he's having a strong reaction to his stepsister's death. I don't think goading and baiting him

160

is the correct approach here, no matter how much you feel he deserves it."

"He deserves it, all right," Amy muttered. "That picture was indecent!" She directed a glare over her shoulder.

"Well, I think the right thing to do now is for you to go and call Bruno Morales. Here's his card." I pulled out the card Bruno had pressed on me Saturday night from the front pocket of my gardening overalls. "There's a pay phone right by the south entrance. You have change?"

She nodded. "You don't think this guy is dangerous, do you?"

"Not at the moment, no." I gave her a little push. "I'll tell him I'm sending you to the library. He won't try anything, I'm sure. But I know Bruno wants to talk to him, and I think he does really need help, which Bruno can advise his family about."

"He's headed for meltdown, you think?" Amy sounded worried. "Is he going to go postal on you?"

"I doubt it, and if he does, I'll whack him with the shovel. If Bruno isn't back in his office yet, leave him a message. I'll smooth this guy down."

"Okay, but after I call I'm coming right back."

"Just don't set him off. You've given him enough food for thought, assuming he's capable of digesting it."

"Yeah, yeah." She strode up the path, pushing past Tom Dancey to head for the gate.

He watched her go with relief, and turned to me.

"She's going to the library for a little while." I gave him a measured look. "Say what you want to say quickly."

"Thanks for talking to me. I know I'm not thinking too straight," he said, his voice low. "I know this is foolish. I know the police think it was an accident. Maybe it was.

Maybe it was." He sighed. "I just don't want her to be dead at all. That's the problem."

"You and your sister were close?"

"She was never my sister," he corrected me. "She called herself that, but I never thought of her as a sister from the moment she came to live at our house. At first she was just a confounded nuisance, and then——"

His eyes slid away, his voice died. "You were dating, I heard?"

"Dating." The harsh laugh seemed forced out of him. "What a word to describe what we did! She was—so out there, so bewitching. I couldn't help myself. I had to give her whatever she wanted. I guess I should have known she'd want her freedom. I even gave her that. But I never stopped loving her. Never."

In the silence that followed his passionate outburst, I could hear the rustle of squirrels in the ivy, checking their winter stores, and the sound of cars whooshing past on Embarcadero Road. Voices called to each other from the cultural center. A businessman, probably on his lunch break, strolled along the perimeter path, looking with enjoyment at the garden plots he passed, and giving Tom Dancey and me a curious glance.

"Did she say anything to make you think someone here at the garden wanted to hurt her?"

His head came up in surprise. I wished I'd never asked the question—that was for Bruno to do, not me. But somehow Dancey seemed ripe for it.

"Yes, she did," he answered, blinking away his confusion. "After she told me . . . after we stopped 'dating' "—his voice surrounded the despised word with quote marks—"she started seeing someone from here."

"Webster?"

162

"Yes, that's the name. Webster something or other. Anyway, she spent more time at the garden then, and once she said to me that something fishy was going on." He flushed a little. "It's no secret that my family has proposed a HUD-sanctioned low-income project for this site, and we're having some trouble getting a determination from the city. She knew I'd be interested in anything that would—tarnish the garden and make housing seem more desirable."

"And you want my help to finish the job?" I tried to keep my voice even, but I was starting to feel a tirade well up within me.

"That doesn't matter anymore," he said, shrugging it off with supreme disinterest. "What does anything matter? She's dead. And she thought something fishy was going on here. Didn't another woman die last night? Seems to me that Rita was right."

I was still hung up on the idea of Rita as treacherous spy for her family's interests. "Didn't it mean anything to Rita that she worked here? She was willing to sell us down the river to developers?"

"Low-income housing is important." Dancey's voice lacked conviction.

"And I suppose your firm is working on a pro bono basis."

"Heck, no," he said, and gave me a watery grin. "Look, this is beside the point. I can't begin to care about it. As far as I'm concerned, this site is only one thing now. Rita's graveyard."

"Tom—" I put out a hand, but he didn't see for a few minutes, sunk in unpalatable thought. I didn't try to interrupt him.

Then he made a visible effort and smiled at me.

Dancey's smile was charming, indeed. Though he was probably no older than my age of mid-thirties, his face was already creased and deeply suntanned. All the melancholy lines rearranged themselves when he smiled, though.

"This was a mistake, I know." He blinked, and his voice firmed. "Maybe I'm brooding too much, keeping too much to myself. If there is anything fishy going on in this garden, I'm not going to find out by pestering the gardeners. But if you hear anything, would you contact me?" He reached in his pocket, and pulled out his hand, empty. He looked at it with vague surprise. "I forgot my cards today. Never mind."

He smiled again, but it didn't quite reach those reddened eyes. I thought he was turning to go, so I started talking to keep him there until Bruno showed up. "Well, the fishiest thing around here normally is just kelp and fish emulsion. But that doesn't mean that there isn't something going on. Unfortunately, the woman who knew the most about everything was the one who died last night after your sister's memorial. I don't know who else you'd ask. Most everyone has told what they knew to the police, so—" I saw with relief that Bruno was rounding the corner of the equipment shed, with Amy trailing along behind him.

Dancey followed the direction of my gaze. "Who is that?" His voice sharpened.

"It's Bruno Morales, the officer in charge of the investigation into these deaths." I waved, and Bruno waved back. "You said you were going to get in touch with him. And here he is! How convenient."

"Very," he muttered, looking suspiciously at me. His hand inside the pocket of his fleece vest clenched.

"Mr. Dancey. So good to finally touch base with you." Bruno charged up, holding out his hand as if in friendly greeting. Dancey was taller and broader, but I would have backed Bruno in a fight.

Dancey shook hands, reluctantly, and Bruno began to pull him along. "I'm parked just over there," he said, leading the way down the garden path. Amy stayed outside the fence until Bruno had taken Dancey through the gate. "Let's go sit in my car. I have much to ask you."

"Fine." The dispirited look settled over Dancey's face. "I've got some questions for you, too."

Amy came over to the plot, where I was quickly packing up the tools. "Wow. Is Bruno arresting that guy?"

"I don't think so. He just wants to talk to him. And I don't think Dancey would have hurt his stepsister. He was—very fond of her."

"He's nutso," Amy said bluntly. "I was kind of afraid to leave you alone in here with him, but Bruno—Mr. Morales—said I should stay at the library until he got there." She shivered. "It would be pretty creepy if he killed her, wouldn't it? I mean, we would have been talking to a murderer." Her eyes grew round. "I could have been slanging a murderer, right to his face!"

"I don't think he is. But if so, we'd better watch out."

"Why?" Amy picked up the shovel and a bucket. "He's been hauled away."

"He's being questioned. He'll be out of Bruno's car after that. And we'll be long gone, so he can't follow us home and continue our conversation."

Amy was silent while we loaded the bus. We hopped in, much to Barker's pleasure, and tooled out of the

165

parking lot, passing Bruno's car on the way. Bruno had been driven over in a cruiser, instead of driving his own car, which meant he expected trouble. He sat in back with Tom Dancey, while Officer Rhea sat in front. It looked like Bruno was taking Dancey very seriously indeed.

"He'll be mad when Bruno lets him go, won't he?" Amy's voice was small. "Won't he, Aunt Liz?"

"Yeah." I turned toward Embarcadero instead of taking Newell to Channing, as I would have if I were on my way straight home. "Yeah, I think he will."

# 20 _____

**PARKING** the bus at the end of my driveway, I saw from the corner of my eye a figure rise up on the front porch. I jammed on the brake faster than I meant to, and Amy's seat belt snapped her back into her seat.

"What—"

Before the panic could blossom, I realized that the majestic figure was Claudia Kaplan, hauling herself out of the fraying wicker chair on the porch. She was clad, as usual, in one of her flowing outfits, and wore her iron-gray hair pulled back in a bun, much as she'd probably worn it when she was an undergraduate years before. Her queenly figure advanced on us when we hopped out of Babe.

"Liz. Oh, I see Amy is visiting. Hello, Amy." She offered a ritual embrace, but bent her commanding gaze on me. "Liz. There's something very strange going on."

"Tell me about it."

"Actually," Claudia said, reflecting briefly, "several strange things. Did you know a woman was parked across your driveway when I got here today?"

"Carlotta."

"You know her?" Claudia's brows bent into a frown. "She babbled some nonsense about watching you. I told

167

her to go away and never come back, so I'm sorry if she's a friend."

"Far from it." I gave Claudia a hug myself. "Thanks for sending her away, but she'll be back. She's stalking me."

Amy turned around. "You said something about being stalked yesterday, Aunt Liz. What is going on here, anyway?"

"I have much the same question." Claudia looked on Amy with approval. "Do you have a few minutes to talk, Liz?"

"Sure. I just want to get this stuff put away." I opened the back of the bus and pulled out the shovel and rake.

Amy took the buckets and unlocked the garage for me. "I'll clean the tools if you want to put the veggies away," she said. "But don't say anything, like, major until I'm there."

Claudia followed me into the kitchen. "Isn't it the middle of the school year? Has Amy transferred out here?"

"Shh." I peered through the window over the sink to make sure Amy was still in the garage. "Don't put such an idea into her head, although it's probably already there. Her school had a fire, so the students are off for a while, and she's doing college visitation here."

Claudia subjected me to the penetrating stare that is characteristic of her. "What's the real reason?"

"Why don't you think that's the real reason?"

"Because her mother didn't come with her." Claudia swept the living room with a comprehensive glance. "Her mother would never have let Amy go off college visiting alone. And there's only one bag here erupting with female apparel. Amy's mother didn't come, so the college visiting is just an excuse."

"Well, you're right, but the real reason is Amy's private business, so I can't tell it."

"She's pregnant." Claudia observed me closely as she made this pronouncement, and then nodded with satisfaction. "She's come here to take care of it. Very sensible. I always thought she had a good head on her shoulders." She paused. "Of course, it's an imposition on you. Will she be staying several months?"

"I don't believe so." Our eyes met for a long moment. "I don't think she's really firmly made up her mind about her course of action. We're just coping with one day at a time." I lifted the little lettuces out of the colander and rolled them in a dish towel, which I tucked into the refrigerator.

"So, this woman who's stalking you. What's that about?"

"You remember her—Carlotta. She lived next door when Vivien was alive."

"I didn't know your Vivien very well, and I don't think I met Carlotta at all." Claudia pulled over a bowl of lady apples on the kitchen table and chose one after careful examination. The apples had been gleaned through an elderly friend of Bridget's who lived in Los Altos Hills. I had permission to pick anything in her orchard, which was no longer plowed and sprayed, but which still gave apricots and plums and peaches and apples in season. The fruit was small and occasionally wormy, but deliciously sweet with a wild tang, excellent for jams and preserves.

"Carlotta is just trying to find something to do with her time, now that she's at the Forum and hasn't got many household chores to keep her busy." I spoke with a degree of dismissal I was far from feeling. Claudia was a

169

powerful weapon; she was not the type to stand by and see a friend troubled. If she decided to take care of Carlotta for me, it could get ugly.

"She had better find something else to do besides bother you," Claudia said, burnishing her chosen apple on her sleeve. She bit into it, her large, white teeth closing with a snap. She had excellent teeth for her age.

"It's nothing. Don't worry about it." I spoke as forcefully as I could. The force rather bounced off Claudia.

Amy came in. "All right. Now, what did that man say?"

Claudia raised her eyebrows. "What man? Is there something else besides your stalker?"

"Is there!" Amy plunged into a rather incoherent account, while I silently cursed the gods who had sent Claudia over on this day of all days. She was immersed in her latest book, which was a definitive biography of Jane Lathrop Stanford that required a ton of reading and a lot of time spent in various Stanford libraries. I had probably seen more of her during the past couple of months than anyone else in her circle, because one of my odd jobs was to do a weekly garden cleanup for her. She pays more than generously, and her garden is an interesting mix, displaying many of her past enthusiasms as well as the plants she is currently involved with.

But her curiosity is exceeded only by her determination to set things right for everyone she cares about. While Amy chattered away about dead people and Bruno Morales and the community garden and Tom Dancey, I waited for Claudia to leap into the whole mess with her usual enthusiasm for detecting, which is accompanied by a touching faith that she can accomplish more than the police, especially Drake, ever could.

She surprised me by saying, when Amy finally sputtered to a halt, "I'm sorry to hear of the deaths. But I'm sure Bruno has it all under control." She sniffed. "It must drive Drake wild to know that his partner is in charge and he can't mess it up."

"Drake doesn't mess things up. He and Bruno work together to solve cases." I couldn't explain why I felt the need to defend Drake. He would have found Claudia's remark merely funny. What rivalry there is comes strictly from her.

"At any rate, interesting as this turmoil in the garden is, it's not the reason I came over." She bent that gaze on me again, the one that turns my knees to jelly and makes me confess even if I didn't do anything. "Liz, I have reason to believe that Bridget is planning a birthday party for me." She paused. "A surprise party."

"As if anyone could plan anything with all this stuff going on." I turned my back on her to scrub baby beets and carrots.

"You've heard nothing about it?" Even without confronting that gimlet stare, I could feel her powerful will reaching out to subject me to mental lie-detector rays. The only defense against this is the blatant sophistry of finding a truthful, even if nonfactual, answer to every question.

"Is today your birthday? I didn't know." I'd thought it was Wednesday. At least, that's what Bridget had said.

"It's Wednesday," she said. "I wouldn't care for a surprise party. If anyone were to give me a birthday party, I would want to look my best, and not like I thought I was going to baby-sit four rowdy children. And I certainly wouldn't want any actual numbers mentioned, in terms of my age."

I didn't dare look at her. "If Bridget knows it's your birthday, you'll get a cake. That's how she is."

"She's asked me to baby-sit for them. I assumed she'd spring dinner on me at the least. And, of course, a cake." Claudia came over to the sink to dispose of her apple core in the compost bucket. She leaned against the counter next to me, intent on her goal. "But will there be people other than the Montroses? Will people take idiotic pictures of me dressed in sweatpants and gaping in surprise? Will I need earplugs to avoid being deafened by loud music? Will there be those terrible little hats with elastic that bites into your chins and makes you look like a lunatic? Will I be required to make a witty speech extempore?" She cleared her throat. "That's the kind of thing I would like to know. I thought you could tell me."

The beets demanded all my attention. I scrubbed furiously. "Well, Claudia, follow the Boy Scout motto in this case. Dress nicely, keep your mouth closed, accept no headgear, and think up some non-extempore wit. Then you'll be ready no matter what happens."

She nodded once. "I see."

"Is there going to be a party?" Amy stopped chomping her own apple long enough to ask.

"I will, no doubt, be the last to know." Claudia turned her formidable attention on Amy. "You are visiting colleges? I know a few people at Santa Clara University and at Stanford. And Berkeley, come to that." She frowned. "My Berkeley friend in the admissions office is retiring next month, so she won't be of any use to you. But if you'd like appointments with faculty in any particular school, I might be able to help you. Otherwise it might be difficult to get interviews on the spur of the minute."

I could see that Amy felt bad for leading Claudia to

think her main purpose in visiting was to check out colleges. It wouldn't have surprised me if she'd just started in and told Claudia everything. Claudia is the sort of person who can extract your story, no matter how personal, in the minimum amount of time. Since I can't keep a secret around her, it is a good thing I have so few secrets.

Amy was made of sterner stuff than I thought, however. She thanked Claudia nicely and said she'd welcome any assistance.

"Come over this afternoon," Claudia said. "After four. I'll write down some phone numbers for you, and make a couple of calls if I have time. What curricula were you planning to check out?"

"Business school, international relations, and mechanical engineering," Amy said promptly.

Claudia blinked. "Well, I believe I can help you in a couple of those disciplines." She moved over to the door. "I know you're busy, Liz, so I won't linger. Let me know if you need some help persuading Carlotta to leave you alone. I'm rather good at that sort of thing, if I do say so myself."

I saw her out the door, and Amy joined me to watch her stride away. "I bet she's good at it," Amy whispered. "She could make me do just about anything."

"It's a useful personality trait," I agreed. "And she doesn't really intimidate her friends. Often."

"Right." Amy turned back to examine the refrigerator. "So there's going to be a surprise party, huh? Did you realize, Aunt Liz, that we haven't had lunch yet?"

"I'm hungry." And I was. It seemed like a long time since breakfast. "Shall I cook these veggies now or save them for dinner?"

"Dinner." Amy didn't even glance at the baby beets, glistening like rubies and topazes. I put them in the crisper. "Peanut butter is fine for lunch."

She made a huge peanut butter and jam sandwich on the homemade bread I'd baked the previous morning. I made a slightly less epic version and put come carrots and celery in a dish on the table.

"Say, I saw a bicycle in the garage, Aunt Liz. Does it work?"

I swallowed peanut butter, not without effort. "Yes, I got it at a garage sale and Drake fixed it up. It's not fancy, but it goes."

"I could ride that to Claudia's," Amy said around her own mouthful. "And maybe leave early and stop on the way to check in at the office." This referred to the stock-brokerage where she'd had a summer job on her previous visit. "I want to hear what the guys there think about the current market. Wanna make sure my college money gets the max."

Hearing Amy talk about college interviews and savings made it pretty clear what course she'd chosen. I didn't ask anything, however. I thought she'd tell me about it when she wanted. And I didn't want to be backed into giving advice. I was still unsure how I felt about it all.

Amy spiffed up a little to visit her buddies at the bro-kerage house—she changed the ragged flannel shirt she wore over her baggy linen jumper for a ragged black sweatshirt, took the helmet I insisted she wear, and pedaled off down the drive. I settled down at my desk, Barker at my feet, and tried to prune my notes on an article about bitter greens for *Organic Gardening* into some semblance of coherent thought. This process wasn't helped by not having an assignment—I'd queried a couple of weeks ago and not heard back yet, so I didn't even know if they'd buy the article. I wondered if the editor had tried to call me at Drake's and failed somehow to leave a message. I wondered if it was time to bow to consensus and get my own phone, even a fax machine. Even an on-line connection for my ancient computer, which probably couldn't begin to handle it.

The speeding bullet of technology is making a Luddite of me. Why should it matter to everyone that they had to leave messages and write letters to contact me? Why did everything have to be done instantaneously? I looked at Charlotte Brontë's *Shirley* on my bookshelf and knew that no one would have the effrontery to write such a book in this day and age. Readers lacked the attention span for Victorian masterpieces; the high moral tone Brontë espoused and her characters' hidden reserves of passion would lack accessibility in the modern age. And the mind-boggling thing is that Brontë wrote it all on tiny scraps of paper while sitting near the fire in the evenings, the only time she had free for authorship. It seemed churlish to complain about lack of telephone and fax machine in the face of that triumph of determination.

All that the cogitation about office equipment accomplished was to keep me from getting very far with my bitter greens article. I had amassed a fair amount of information on the medicinal properties of mustard and corn mâche, of radicchio and arugula, and had to weave that material into the article without boring my reader to death. I didn't much relish the task, but it was more appealing than the alternative, which was to go out and find a regular job, working amid all the complicated machines that populate the modern office.

Too scary. I looked at my elderly computer, so old that its sheer bulk occupied major space. In such an unintimidating environment, I should be able to compose a positive epic about bitter greens.

# 21

**THE** knock on my door came before I'd managed to put myself totally to sleep droning on about phytochemicals.

I looked through the window and saw Tamiko standing on the front porch. Huddled into a thick zippered sweater and a skirt, without garden gloves, she looked different.

I opened the door for her. "Hi, Tamiko." She came in hesitantly.

"You must wonder why I'm here." She glanced around, taking in my house. I wished that Amy had thought to pick up the clothes she'd pawed through to find her jacket.

"Not at all," I lied politely. "I almost didn't recognize you without some dirt under your fingernails."

She smiled, but sobered immediately. "Do you have a minute to talk?"

"Sure." I gestured her into the kitchen, away from the hurricane of Amy's personal possessions that cluttered the living room. "Would you like some tea?"

"Yes, thank you." She watched while I put the kettle on and warmed a pot. I spooned in some of my favorite blend of lemon balm, peppermint, and pineapple sage.

When I set the teapot, cups, and honey on the table,

she spoke. "You probably know this is about Lois's death. And Rita's, of course."

"I wondered." I gave the tea a stir and tucked a cozy around it.

"You have the ear of the man who's investigating. Detective Morales."

"Yes, to some extent. So do you, Tamiko. If you have something you want him to know, call and talk to him or leave a message. He wants to hear anything you have to tell."

"This is not something I know." Tamiko leaned forward. "It is only something I wonder about. Have you noticed the stranger, Liz?"

I was pouring the tea, and her words took me by surprise. Some of the fragrant blend splashed on the tabletop. "I'll get it," I said, grabbing a tea towel. "What stranger do you mean?"

"The man who walks around the garden. About noon, a couple of times a week. He wears an overcoat and a hat, and regular shoes—not tennis shoes." Tamiko stuck out one sneaker-clad foot. "I have seen him a couple of times a week for the past month or so. Suddenly today I wondered if he had something to do with their deaths. Rita and Lois."

I remembered the man strolling at the garden while Amy and I worked. "I've seen that guy—he was there today. Maybe he's just some businessman who likes to walk around the garden after lunch."

"He lingers," Tamiko insisted, accepting the cup I put in front of her. I added honey to mine; honey brings out the sweetness of the herbs, and blends their flavors together. "Especially around the gate near our plots, I've noticed. And around the wood chips. Maybe he plans to pull women over behind the wood chips where Lois was found and—"

We stared at each other. "Lois wasn't raped," I said. "And neither was Rita."

"Do you think Detective Morales would be interested in this?" Tamiko took a sip of tea and hastily put the cup down.

"I'll mention it, and I'll tell him you've seen the man a couple of times a week. But I don't think it means anything, Tamiko. There are lots of people walking around there all the time. The woman with the golden retrievers, the man with the big shepherd—"

"And the woman in the blue jogging suit who runs very slowly and listens to headphones." Tamiko nodded. "But they are doing something. This man is doing nothing. Why is he there?"

"Bruno will check it out. He's looking for any information he can find." I hesitated, wondering how to bring up the quarrel Bridget had overheard between her and Rita. And then wondering why I thought it was my business to ask.

Tamiko mentioned it herself. "Mr. Morales has already spoken with me. He heard that I quarreled with Rita." She shot me a glance. "You had heard this, too?"

"Not from Bruno." It made me uneasy to receive her confidence, given that I had no official standing in the investigation. And despite what Drake believed, I had no desire to get involved. I could have been happy if Tamiko had never dropped in, but had gone straight to Bruno with her concerns.

"We quarreled because she wished to blackmail me." Tamiko's voice was expressionless. "I wonder now if she dealt with others through blackmail."

"How could she blackmail you?" I blurted the question out, and then hastened to add, "Never mind. I don't want to know."

Tamiko went on talking in her deliberate way. "It was very simple. She noticed the address on the check I used to pay my garden rent. It is the same as that of one of her friends from high school. She knows—knew—the friend's mother is a lesbian." She glanced at me and then back down at her hands. "Rita said she would tell everyone of my—preferences—if I made any more trouble over the raspberries or the Roundup incident."

"So Rita tried to force you to go along with what she wanted?"

"Yes." Tamiko did not look up. "I am a teacher. And— I am not yet ready to have my private life revealed to the world." She smiled a little. "Not that the world would pay much attention. But Rita's way of doing such a thing would be ugly. It might have made a difference among my coworkers. I do not wish to go through that."

"And you told her—"

"I told her that the job of garden coordinator didn't give her the right to blackmail the gardeners. That made her angry, and then I got angry, too." Tamiko looked up from her hands. "I don't remember exactly what I said. But it was something bad, I know—along the lines of, 'You will get yours.' Ten minutes later she was dead."

We were silent for a moment. I knew that Tamiko, who treated each seedling with the utmost care, was not the kind of woman to take a life. But anyone can be enraged, goaded, until they lash out and push, not meaning to kill, just giving way to their anger and fear.

I just couldn't believe that it had happened that way—

not with Tamiko. "So you think she might have been using those tactics on others besides you?"

Tamiko shrugged. "She and Lois were definitely engaged in a power struggle. Lois threatened to make a big issue out of Rita's conflict of interest—her relationship with the contractor who wanted to build on the site. And Rita was threatening Lois with some statute about unlawful burial."

It was like lifting the lid of the cookie jar and finding baby alligators. "I never knew this stuff was happening. It can't be the same garden I've worked in for three years."

"It is. The garden changes, just like everything else. It will change again now that Rita is gone." Tamiko patted my arm. "You are an idealist, Liz. You do not see the struggle between the earthworm and the nematode. But it is there. Rita was not suitable as a leader for the garden. She could make nothing grow."

"She had a stifling kind of a way with her, that's for sure." I felt dazed. "So you could be right. She could have been using the blackmail approach on other people."

"Those in her personal life, too."

"I hadn't even thought of that. And you say you told all this to Bruno?"

"I told him what passed between Rita and me. But I have only just now begun to wonder about who else she might have tried to blackmail. If you think Detective Morales is interested in my unformed thoughts, I will let him know." Tamiko got up. "Oh, by the way."

"Yes?"

She fidgeted nervously with the zipper tab on her sweater, pulling it up and then back down.

"I have been asked to be the new volunteer coordinator," she said, glancing at me and then away. Her olive skin was warmed to dark rose by an embarrassed blush.

"That's great. You'll do a wonderful job."

"Thank you, Liz." She smiled suddenly, the mischief making her look years younger. "I will notice now when you don't share in the work days. So see that you do."

"Yes, ma'am." I showed her out and went back to my bitter greens, but they failed to occupy me. Instead I went over what Tamiko had said, and it finally occurred to me to wonder just why she'd come by to say it. Her questions about the noonday businessman stroller had simply been a pretext for bending my ear about Rita's blackmailing propensities.

Why me? That's what I couldn't figure out. What did Tamiko have to gain by telling me all of that? I could understand her feeling of being under suspicion, her need to justify herself.

I couldn't help but wonder, though, why she chose me as her confidant. She could have gone to Bruno without my advice. In fact, I would have expected her to.

Now she was volunteer coordinator. Maybe she'd wanted the post all along.

I didn't like these thoughts. I refused to let them link up in my head any longer. But I couldn't altogether chase them away.

# 22 _____

I gave up working and stared out the window at the pink glow of sunset. Tamiko had given me too much food for thought; I was choking on the fiber. The possibility that Rita and Lois died natural deaths was growing more and more remote. I could more easily understand violence stalking a woman like Rita. But Lois, with her shrine and her ashes, seemed a totally unlikely victim. Unless someone had wanted something she had. Like the volunteer coordinator position.

The dusk had faded into full darkness when I roused from my thoughts enough to pay attention to Barker's increasingly insistent nose nudges. I gave him food and water, and wondered where Amy was. It was nearly six. I didn't like to think of her biking in the dark with only my bicycle's feeble headlight.

I went to Drake's to call Claudia. Every time I stuck my key in his door, a wave of missing him washed over me. I wanted to find him in his kitchen, the light glinting off his granny glasses, his hair wild with some enthusiasm or other. Instead his house was dark and empty. The air was chilly and felt damp. I turned up the heat to dry things out, and because the chill was too disturbing.

Claudia's voice was absentminded when she answered.

"Hi, it's me, Liz. Is Amy still there?"

"Oh, Liz. No, she's not. She left an hour or more ago. I gave her some materials and made a couple of phone calls, and she's going to do the rest." Her voice sharpened. "She isn't home yet?"

"No. But she probably just stopped downtown. She has some friends around here—maybe she met someone."

"You must be using Drake's phone. Too bad you don't have your own, and Amy could let you know."

"Well, call me an anachronism, but the world got along fine without telephones for billions and billions of years."

In the face of my impatience, Claudia was silent for a moment. She finally spoke with uncharacteristic meekness. "Should I drive around and look for her?"

I was touched. "No, no. She'll be back pretty soon. If anyone drives anywhere, it should be me."

I felt apprehensive all the same. Surely Amy wouldn't go anywhere near the garden alone, and in the dark. She was simply hanging around one of the coffee places downtown with some of her friends from summer.

I told Claudia I would keep her posted and hung up. Then I noticed the message light glinting on the answering machine.

The message was from Drake. "Liz, sorry I won't be able to call tonight. Something's come up. I'll leave another message or call when I can." Then came a quick jumble of words I couldn't quite make out—he sounded weary in the extreme. But I thought he was saying, "I love you."

His father, I guessed, wasn't doing well.

I glared at the telephone. It was a loathsome monster, bringer of hideous news and dreadful uncertainty.

I wanted to sit next to it until it rang again and I heard Drake's voice.

Instead, I locked the door with careful precision and started toward my house, wondering if I should get into Babe and cruise the cafés. I felt the weight of my inexperience as an in-lieu parent. Amy was old enough and smart enough to take care of herself in a benign place like Palo Alto. A place, I reminded myself, where two women had recently died in suspicious circumstances.

Gravel rattled in the driveway. Amy wheeled the bike past Drake's house, trudging beside it, her head down. She didn't see me till I spoke.

"Amy, are you all right? Did you fall?"

"Huh?" She lifted her head and stared at me. In the light from the kitchen window, I could see the stunned bewilderment on her face.

"What's happened?" I ran down the steps and took the bike, propping it against the garage door. When I put my arm around her, she broke into sobs.

I hugged her, though I had to stand on tiptoe to do it—she tops me by a good four inches. "What is it? What happened? Are you hurt?"

Gulping, she shook her head. I guided her toward the house. For once I was without a handkerchief or bandanna in my pocket. But I had a drawer full of them inside.

Amy sat at the kitchen table. Her hands and cheeks were cold, so I put the kettle on and found her a hankie. She was trying to stop crying, but sobs kept bursting out in the most heartrending way.

I got out the chamomile tea and made a pot. We could both use some calming down.

The aroma of the tea steadied Amy. She cradled her cup and stared into it as she spoke.

"I was just biking home after going to Mrs. Kaplan's house." Amy gulped back a sob. "She—was very nice and got me stuff about college. Anyway, I was going down University Avenue so I could see if I knew anybody. And while I was at a stoplight that man came by."

"What man? Tom Dancey?"

Amy nodded. "He didn't seem mad at all—thanked me for letting the police know, said he felt better after talking to Mr. Morales. Then he apologized for this morning. He—he seemed very down, and when the light turned green he walked across with me. And he—he started talking about how I must know I couldn't kill anything, how bad it would be to kill my"—she glanced at her stomach with fearful fascination—"my baby. How it deserved to live just like I did. I—I wanted to get away, but he was very quiet and reasonable and I just couldn't ride away. See, that stepsister or whatever she was had an abortion, and he's really torn up about it, and he has this mission now to save babies." She looked at me, her eyes welling with tears. "And it's no good, Aunt Liz. I don't want this baby, but I can't get rid of it, like—like a weed or something."

I stared back at her. "So, what are you saying here?"

"I don't know." The words were a wail. "I don't know what to do. I thought I did, but now it's all changed. I mean, before, I didn't really think about it as a real baby, a real person in there. What if it was me? What if Mom had gotten rid of me?"

186

"Instead of marrying Andy, you mean?" I was too dazed to realize I'd let a family skeleton out of the closet until Amy pounced on my words.

"I thought so," she said triumphantly. "I asked Mom, one time, why my birthday was only seven months after their wedding date, and she said I was premature. But I could tell, the way she looked. I knew they had to get married because of me."

"Well, they did get married. Your mom didn't have to raise you alone and provide for you alone," I pointed out, trying to lend some balance to the situation. "And she and Andy definitely did the deed. You didn't, really."

"I was just as stupid as if I did," Amy muttered. "Going to a party with dumb guys like that, just to get drunk. I was asking for it."

Since I pretty much agreed with her, I fumbled for something to say. "You weren't the only one in that hot tub. That boy behaved very badly indeed. Everybody makes mistakes, honey. Yours wasn't such a big one."

"But it resulted in a big problem." Amy looked at her stomach again. "I certainly don't want to keep the baby. Every time I saw it I would think of that cretin who got me into this." Her voice dripped scorn. "But someone else might want it. I guess I'll have to have it and give it away."

"Lots of people want to adopt." I sipped my tea, preparing myself for what I knew would come.

"Aunt Liz," Amy said pleadingly. "Can I stay here? I'll go to school. I'll behave. But I just can't be pregnant and go back home. They—they might make me marry that moron." Her eyes filled again with tears. "Mom—she would be so—disappointed," she wailed. "She told me and told me—"

The thought of Renee confronted with the shame of her only child boggled the mind. "But, Amy. If you're going to have the baby, you'll have to tell them you're pregnant. And do you really think Renee would let you spend the whole school year here? I mean, they are your parents."

"Oh, God." Amy jumped up, looking around in a hunted fashion. "I've got to think. I just can't seem to think!"

"Why don't you rest in my room? I'll make some dinner."

She gave me a quick hug. "I'm so sorry. This is just a total bummer!" Then she disappeared into my bedroom and closed the door.

I stared around the living room of my little cottage in dismay. Amy's traces were everywhere—her carpetbag spilling out clothes in the corner, her makeup case and hair dryer on the piecrust table, her radio on the floor by the couch, along with several of the sofa cushions. She had put the sleeper part of the couch back that morning, at least. But I wondered if we could both stand to live in such closer quarters for months on end. I value my privacy, and Amy, though sweet, is not particularly retiring.

I put a big pot of water on for pasta. And then I went back across the yard to Drake's house. Luckily Bridget was home.

"It's me, Liz."

"Liz. Where are you calling from? Oh, you must be at Drake's. Is he back?" Bridget sounded cheerful. I could hear clattering in the background and knew she was cooking dinner with the phone tucked between her ear and shoulder, as I'd seen it so often before.

"No, he's not back. But Amy's having—a bit of a crisis. She's been listening to the antiabortion side and now she thinks she wants to have the baby and give it up for adoption. Would you have time to stop by this evening and talk to her? She's so confused, and I don't feel capable of handling this."

Bridget was silent for a moment. "Of course, I'll come by if you want me to, Liz. And if it will help. But I can't take sides here, and neither should you. It seems to me that the concept of choice requires that women make a decision for themselves. Amy shouldn't be any more swayed by the pro-lifers than by anyone else. In the end, it comes down to her own personal decision. And I'm glad to hear that she's taking it very seriously. It's a serious subject."

Once more Bridget had surprised me. I had expected a woman with four young children to have more forcible views.

"Well, I think it would help her if you could come by. What do I know about the fix she's in? Neither of us knows anything about the reality of childbirth or child-rearing."

"Okay," Bridget agreed. "But after dinner, all right?"

"That's fine. I'm just making dinner now. Do you want to come over here and share ours?"

She laughed. "I'd love to, but I'd better stay home and give my family theirs. I'll drop in around eight, after Moira and Mick are in bed."

I felt better after I hung up the phone. I didn't expect Bridget to make up Amy's mind for her. But I didn't like to see Amy in so much anguish, and I wasn't sure I knew what to say.

There were no new messages on the answering machine.

I lingered for a minute, trying to make the telephone ring with a call from Drake. It kept silent, the disobliging thing.

I locked up again and went to cook pasta.

# 23 _____

**GETTING** those lovely little beets and greens out of the fridge made me feel somewhat better. I steamed the beets and stir-fried their tender greens in olive oil and garlic, along with some mushrooms I'd traded salad mix for at the farmers' market. When the pasta was cooked I tossed it all together with some Parmesan cheese and went to call Amy.

She was lying on her back on my bed. The quilt was scrunched up under her, and a big, damp splotch on one pillowcase showed that she'd been crying. She'd stopped, though.

"Dinner's ready."

"That's great." She got up and pulled ineffectually at the quilt. "I've messed up your bed, Aunt Liz. I'm sorry. You keep everything so tidy. . . ." Her voice trailed off.

"Do you want to wash your face?"

"Good idea." She disappeared into the bathroom, and I went to arrange the food as attractively as I could.

A few minutes later she came into the kitchen and handed me a loaf of sourdough bread. "I forgot about this. I got it when I went down to the brokerage house, before going to Mrs. Kaplan's."

"Thanks, Amy. That was nice." I sliced some of the

bread and thought we might have the rest as French toast in the next couple of days. Amy sat down listlessly. "How was the brokerage?"

"A bunch of people had left." She used her fork to poke the pasta. "What all's in this?"

"Stuff we got at the garden this morning. Baby beets and beet greens, and mushrooms, cheese—"

"Sounds good." She took a bite, and then another. "Guess I'm going to have to start eating for two."

"I asked Bridget to come by later. I thought you might find it helpful to talk to her."

Amy sighed. "There's just no getting around it, Aunt Liz. Believe me, I've thought and thought."

"Well, you don't have to talk about it if you don't want to."

Amy pushed her plate aside. "Aunt Liz, I know I shouldn't ask you if I can stay here. But if I can—if I can make it all right with Mom and get into school, will you let me stay? I promise I'll do my share and I'll get a job and help out with the groceries—"

She was getting choked up again.

"Amy. Take it easy. If you can make it all right with your parents, you're welcome to stay." I told myself this wasn't a lie. I did welcome her. I just welcomed my privacy more. But a relative in trouble takes precedence over all the privacy in the world.

"Thanks." She swallowed her emotions and gave me a smile. "Thanks a lot. I promise, you won't regret it."

Then the smile faded. She ate mechanically, not even tasting the succulent sweetness of those wonderful beets. Perhaps it is a sign of my insensitive nature, but in the course of my life, I've had to eat food that could only be choked down if a person was very, very hungry. Now if something tastes extra good, I can't help but appreciate it.

We got the kitchen cleaned up before Bridget arrived. She brought with her a pan of apple crisp, still warm, carried in a basket. "I made a little one for you all since I was making a big one for us," she explained, setting the basket on the table. "Can you tell I bought a bushel of apples recently? You can save it for later if you're full."

"No one smelling that could be full." Amy perked up. "Can I get some for you, Mrs. Montrose? Aunt Liz?"

Bridget shook her head and sat at the table. "No, but if you're going to make tea, I'll take some of that. And please call me Bridget, Amy. When I hear Mrs. Montrose, I think I'm on classroom helper duty."

While Amy filled the kettle, I gave Bridget an inquiring look, and she responded with a tiny jerk of her head toward the door. "Actually," I said, raising my voice to be heard above the water, "I'm going to run over to Drake's for a while until he calls."

"Okay." Amy didn't seem to care. Perhaps she'd speak more freely to Bridget than to me, fearing that I would eventually have to tell her parents anything she confided.

There were no new messages on Drake's answering machine. I rummaged through the CDs piled on top of the bookcase that held his sound equipment and found one of Sting's, whom I vaguely recalled seeing in the glossy gossip magazine at the clinic that morning. I wandered through the living room as the music spilled into the air, touching the backs of the chairs, trying to imagine that I lived there with Drake.

My imagination couldn't do the trick. I paused in the doorway to Drake's bedroom. I could see us together—even in that room, in his big, modern bed that he straightened by the simple expedient of pulling up the sheet and flapping a comforter over it all. The thought of sharing his bed made my face heat up. It had been so long since I'd wanted to feel what I was feeling for Drake. So long since I had trusted a man to treat my feelings with tenderness.

I picked up one of his pillows and hugged it to me, a display of maudlin behavior it shames me to recount. It smelled like him. I buried my face in it and wished someone would grant me the power of knowing what was best to do. But it seemed to me that there was no decision to make—at this point, no turning back. Drake and I would end up in this bed together, probably very soon after he returned—unless he didn't return. If he stayed in Seattle—I didn't want to think about that. But becoming lovers wouldn't stop him from pushing me. He'd want me to move in with him. He'd mentioned marriage.

I just couldn't make that leap. The here and now was scary enough for me. Trying to second-guess the future was next to impossible. I could only see myself, huddled in my little house, protecting the frail shelter of the life I'd built. It was unthinkable to give that up for the even more uncertain territory of building a life with Drake.

The phone rang. I tossed the pillow back on the bed and ran for it.

"Liz." Drake sounded exhausted. "You're there. I was just going to leave a message."

"You're tired. We don't have to talk if you don't want to."

"It's the only thing I want right now. Well, not the only thing—" His voice softened. My face warmed again.

"How's your dad?"

"Did the marrow transplant today. Something made him have a bad reaction. He barely made it through."

"Oh, no."

"He's better now. In fact, the doctors think that was the worst of it. My mom—" He hesitated. "She's worn out. My sister took her home. I'm staying here tonight."

"Will you get some rest?"

"I'd conk out right now if you just sing a little lullaby." He laughed. "I'll sleep. But we're all wearing out. I swear, I don't think he'd live through another episode of this. It's so hard to be caught between living and dying."

"Oh, Paul."

"What's happening there?" He yawned. "I didn't get my e-mail today. Bruno handling everything?"

"Yeah. He's moving along." I debated telling him what I knew about the investigation so far, but what was the use? He was miles away and preoccupied. Anything he wanted to know, he could get from Bruno. "Amy's thinking about having the baby and giving it up for adoption."

"Don't tell me. She wants to stay with you until it's over." He sounded resigned.

"Yep. Liz's home for unwed mothers. That's what I'll be running."

"You don't have to let her impose like that."

"Yes, I do."

He was quiet. "Guess you do, at that. Poor thing."

I didn't ask if the sympathy was for me or Amy. "We managed okay last summer. But I might get a regular bed for her. I don't think that Hide-A-Bed is comfortable."

"Is this okay with her parents?"

"If it isn't, she can't stay. I already told her that."

"You're a nice person, Ms. Sullivan. Have I ever told you that?"

"I believe you've mentioned it. Takes one to know one."

He laughed again. "You're flirting with me."

"No, can't be. I don't know how."

"Well, don't practice with anyone else." Another yawn. "I'm going to have to hit the sack."

"Sleep well. I'll send positive vibrations to your dad."

"You do that."

I cradled the phone, still smiling. Bridget's knock on the back door startled me. I must have jumped a foot.

"Were you talking to Drake?" She opened the door and came in, looking at me curiously. "I waited until you hung up."

"Yeah, he called. What about your talk?"

Bridget shrugged. "We just chatted. I gave her another book—*To Love and Let Go,* by Suzanne Arms. She's worried about the health risks of pregnancy, which are very real even for young people like her. And childbirth is very painful and also can be dangerous. It's important to weigh it all. The man who wants her to have this baby—he's got no idea of what she would have to go through."

"Well, I don't think she's really made up her mind." I turned off the kitchen light and ushered Bridget out. "And it's certainly something to think deeply about, for sure. She'll do what's right for her, once she's turned it all over."

"She's pretty levelheaded for a girl that age." Bridget had her empty basket over her arm.

"Are you walking home alone in the dark?"

"Two whole blocks." She grinned, her teeth flashing white in the moonlight.

"I'll get Barker and go with you. He's dying for a walk."

Amy was listening to the radio while she read the book Bridget had brought. I told her where I was going, and she rubbed Barker's ears. "Barker will be glad. He's antsy tonight, aren't you, big boy?"

I got the leash on him, even though he was dancing around. "Say," Amy added as an afterthought, "I left my jean jacket at your garden plot. Do you think it'll still be there?"

"It'll be there tomorrow morning if it's there tonight," I said. "I'm not going there until daylight."

"Guess that's a good idea. Maybe I'll jog Barker over tomorrow and get it." Amy glanced down at her stomach, with that expression of mingled horror and fascination she'd been wearing all evening. "I don't want to get fat. My friend Louise's sister had a baby and she still looks pregnant after a year. That can't happen to me."

"Tell you what. I'll go for a morning swim, then go over to the garden and put in those potatoes I forgot today. You can jog Barker over and meet me there."

She turned back to her book and I wrestled Barker out the door.

Bridget had been walking around the yard, rubbing a leaf of the rose-scented geranium between her fingers. "Your garden is so nice, even at this time of year," she marveled.

"At night you can't see all the bad places." I had neglected my daily chores in the raised beds that day.

"I see it in daylight all the time, and I still think so." She walked beside me down the drive. Barker strained at the leash. I had to speak to him sharply. "It's a million times better than my yard. When Moira gets to be ten, I'll have some landscaping done. But they just kill everything now, not that they mean to, but flower beds look like mudpie vats to them, and trees are just climbing frames or sources of sticks, and Mick pulled all the flowers off my Shasta daisy to make me a bouquet. My yard is hopeless."

I agreed with that. "Your kids have fun, though. People with those manicured lawns, you never see their children playing there."

"They do have fun. They drive me crazy, but they enjoy it."

"Have you finished your next book yet?"

Bridget looked around as if someone might hear her. "I can't even start it," she whispered. "Until the first one comes out and people buy it. I know I should be writing away and have the next one ready, like Claudia tells me to, but I can't."

"Well, you have Moira, too. Child-tending is a full-time occupation." I had found that out for myself while sitting for Bridget.

"It makes a good excuse anyway."

We were at Bridget's house. From the sidewalk, it looked homey and comfortable, with light streaming from the living room windows. I could just see Emery's red head bent over a book.

"Thanks for coming, and for the apple crisp."

"Thanks for the escort." She eyed Barker. "I guess he's enough guard for you."

"Certainly if anyone attacked me, he'd slobber them into running away."

On the walk back, I didn't feel as safe as I wanted to. I had the uneasy feeling of being followed. Finally I gave in and turned around. Carlotta was behind me.

Barker pranced toward her. "Call off your dog," Carlotta shrieked.

"He's not on yet. If you bother me, I'll let him off the leash."

"I'm not going to bother you." She sounded breathless. "I just wanted to tell you—you don't have to worry about me anymore."

"I wasn't worried about you in the first place."

"I have decided it's the police's job to keep tabs on you." She sounded very prim and proper. "I shall just wait for them to deal with it."

"Much the best policy. And don't bother coming to the writers' workshop tomorrow or any day, Carlotta. You aren't welcome."

"Hmph." She scowled. "We'll see about that." She marched across the street and climbed into her big car.

Barker and I went on home.

# 24

**AMY** was still reading when I got back. We spent the evening quietly. I gave up on writing and got deeper into *Shirley*.

I woke early the next morning with the thought of swimming foremost in my mind. It would be a busy day, teaching the writers' workshop that afternoon at the senior center. I would need to get my exercise early. After eating a little cereal and working among the raised beds, I got my swimming stuff together.

Amy was up by then, munching a piece of toast thickly spread with blackberry jam. "It's winter, Aunt Liz." She glanced out the window over the sink. "The sun's not even shining. How can you swim outside in this weather?"

"The water's warm."

She didn't look convinced. "I can't imagine swimming outside in the winter. At home, we've had killing frosts since late September." She munched a little more. "So I thought I'd clean the bathroom this morning, and then take Barker for that run. I'd like to get some exercise."

"Is it okay for you to run?"

"I guess. All the books seem to say, just do what you've been doing, and I was on the track team at school." She stretched. Her cropped sweatshirt and low-slung jeans revealed no signs of pregnancy that I could see. "And Barker would like to run, I bet."

"He certainly would."

She swallowed the last bite of toast. "So I'll meet you at the garden. I'll help you plant potatoes, if you can give me a ride back?" She looked a little sheepish. "I haven't worked out for over a week. Don't want to overdo."

While Amy rooted around under the sink for cleaning supplies, I loaded up the seed potatoes and my shovel and garden basket, and drove off to the pool.

The water was warm. I swam freestyle, enjoying the smooth rotation of my body from side to side, following the stroke. The overachiever in the next lane had finished her kickboarding and gotten out, leaving the pool to me. It was still chilly and overcast, and people didn't exactly flock to swim under those circumstances.

Switching to sidestroke, I checked out the gloomy sky. It wouldn't rain, I thought, but it probably wouldn't lift anytime soon. I didn't want it to rain before I was finished planting potatoes.

I pictured Amy giving the old high-sided clawfoot tub a good scrubbing, and had to smile. It had surprised me when she'd volunteered, since I knew cleaning the bathroom wasn't her favorite thing. But she was out to show me what a good roommate she'd make. It was touching. I knew the next seven months would be harder on her than on me. All I lost was my privacy. She was leaving her girlhood behind her for the difficult and painful choices of adulthood.

The lifeguard came over to warn me that it was time to get out. I went into the locker room for one of the ferocious showers that didn't just rinse away the chlorine but blasted it off the face of the planet. The kickboarding woman was pulling on panty hose when I went into the shower area; she was blow-drying her hair when I came out, and checking her look in the mirror. Her look was formidable, from smoothly arranged hair to aggressive black shoes.

I put on jeans, turtleneck, and sweatshirt, all of which had been purchased at that emporium of the people, Goodwill. Probably my whole outfit, including sale-table walking shoes, had cost less than the other woman's high heels. Toweling excess water out of my hair, I thanked my lucky stars for my good fortune in wearing warm, comfortable clothing with no holes in it. I wouldn't trade my life for Ms. Power Suit's, even if hers came complete with a whole closet full of shoes.

I put my swim gear away in Babe and checked that there was water in the reservoir to fill Barker's traveling water dish when he arrived panting at the garden later. Then I drove the short distance around the library to the parking lot.

Carrying the bucket, the bag of seed potatoes, and the spade, I trudged through oak trees toward the garden's south gate. With my head down, I didn't see the man coming out until I nearly ran into him.

"Watch out," he said, trying to step around me and getting tangled in one of the rosebushes that lined the parking lot.

"Sorry." I shifted the spade so it didn't stick out in front of me like a plebeian lance. It was the man Tamiko had mentioned, who'd been strolling around the garden the day before. His overcoat was open, showing the suit and tie beneath. He wore dark glasses, even on this sunless day. After pushing through the bushes, he walked rapidly away, giving me time to notice that he carried a briefcase and had a bald spot on the back of his scalp, the pathetic kind with long strands of hair combed across it. He slung his briefcase into the backseat of a white compact car with a Hertz bumper sticker, and drove away.

I stared after him for a moment, wondering if I should go call Bruno. But the man was gone, and aside from being rude he hadn't seemed dangerous.

Juggling my load, I got everything through the gate. Amy's jacket was draped over the frame of my homemade compost bin, where she'd left it the previous day. The bin was full of stuff I'd crammed in over the past week or so while doing fall cleanup. After moving Amy's jacket, I spent a few minutes with the spade, stirring up the compost so it would cook faster. Of course, an open wire bin was not going to cook very fast at all, especially in the winter. I glanced enviously at Webster's black plastic compost bin. He'd left his gloves on top again, but not neatly disposed as I'd seen them before; they were tumbled together, as if someone had lifted the bin's top hatch to get inside without removing the gloves first.

Staring at Webster's compost bin, I tried to shrug off the mental image I'd gotten, of the man in the suit reaching across the fence, lifting the top hatch of Webster's bin, reaching in—

The man, I told my overactive imagination sternly, was nothing more than an office worker who liked to drive over and take a constitutional around the garden when he wanted to clear his head. But why walk around a garden with a briefcase? Why drive a rental car, come to that?

A formation of geese flew eastward overhead, aiming for the Baylands. The wind blew through the dying leaves.

No one else was around that I could see. I left the spade stuck in the potato bed and walked over to Webster's plot.

His compost bin, right by the perimeter fence, would be easy enough to access from outside the garden. I walked down the center path, past fava beans and broccoli plants, past the wheelbarrow loaded with bagged steer manure and soil conditioner. Putting the gloves aside, I lifted the top hatch of the composter.

The thick smell of decomposing vegetation greeted me, wafted upward on a gust of warm air. Even without sun, the black plastic trapped the heat of decay. Just below the hatch, on the surface of the compost, reposed a metal tray. The tray held a folded piece of paper encased in a Ziploc bag.

This bizarre scene was none of my business. That's what I told myself while I stared at the paper. I didn't make a conscious decision; my hand was reaching for it before I had convinced myself to butt out.

The note was brief, typed or word-processed on a single sheet of white paper folded in half, then into thirds. "We paid. Where is the disk?"

I refolded it and replaced it in the bag and returned it to the metal tray, precisely as it had been. I shut the lid of the compost bin and made sure the gloves were in the same crumpled position I had first seen.

When I turned around, Webster was standing at the end of the path into his garden, watching me.

He didn't say anything. I cleared my throat. "Someone's sending you messages in your compost, Webster."

"Is that so?" He didn't move, but an air of menace came off him, as palpable as the odor of rot from his compost bin.

"Yes. I noticed that your gloves were all messed up,

and took a peek inside. Looks like someone mistook your compost bin for a mailbox."

His smile was brief and cold. "Don't bother, Liz. I've been watching you since you got here. I saw you read the note."

"My curiosity got the better of me. Sorry."

"I'm sure you are." He strolled up the path. "I'm sure you will be. What did the note say?"

I blinked, hoping I looked stupid. "It wasn't interesting. Something about a disk."

He came closer, brushed past me. He was no longer blocking the path, so I edged down it toward the main path. If I ran over his beautiful raised beds, through the raspberry canes and Tamiko's winter vegetables, I could get to the gate. But could I get through it? He was much taller than I, with long legs that would catch me in no time. And I still wasn't sure that I needed to run.

Webster didn't just open the hatch of the compost bin—he took off the whole top, and set it on the ground against the fence. He looked into the bin, then at me. "I didn't have you pegged for the busybody type, Liz. Thought Lois was the only one of those we had around here."

"I'm not a busybody. What you do in your compost bin is your business, not mine."

"So right." He straightened, looking at me with a considering expression. "So you'll keep quiet."

"Of course. It's not like it's fascinating, or anything."

He moved forward, edging me toward the main path. "Tell me, Liz, aren't you just a little nervous about coming here alone after two women have had fatal accidents here?"

"I'm not really alone," I said, gaining the main path

and stepping into my own garden. "I mean, I'm expecting Bruno Morales at any time. He wanted me to meet him here."

"Is that so?" Webster looked amused. "You know, I don't believe that. The only person you're likely to meet here is that nosy Bridget. She's probably busy with her repellent offspring right now."

I stared at the unpleasant sneer on his face. If only Amy and Barker had been there earlier, I would never have succumbed to curiosity. And now she would turn up at the wrong time and get into trouble.

"You're right. No one's coming." I spoke fast, trying to keep his attention focused on me, so he might not notice if Amy rounded the corner of the equipment shed. "No one at all."

His face changed. "So your friend is coming. Or that young woman who was with you yesterday." He watched my face while he said this, and I did my best to look blank, but it wasn't good enough. "Damn."

I edged back, heading for the shovel I'd stuck in the ground. But Webster moved faster. He took one stride and grabbed my arm, dragging me back into the main path.

"I'll have to take care of you now."

"What the hell are you doing, Webster?" I twisted, trying to break his grip, but he was strong.

"I'm going to have to dispose of you, Liz." He sounded aggrieved. "Nothing is going like I planned it."

"You planned to kill Rita and Lois?"

"No, of course not." Great. Now he was offended. "It was all an accident. Rita was—she was out of control. Bleeding me for cash. She was so greedy." He seemed incredulous. "Saying I'd better pay up or she'd see me in jail. She wanted me to give her the next payment that

206

day, the work day. But I was tired of paying. It was my money. Why should she get it when I ran all the risk? I pushed her, and she stumbled back, and then I pushed her again, and she fell over that rake and hit her neck—" His grip on me slackened, and I managed to tear my arm away. But he reached out with his long arm and snagged me again.

"And Lois? What happened to her?"

"She figured out that I had something to do with Rita's death. She told me that night that she knew what I was up to, that Rita had said something about it. I could see that she was bluffing, but if questions were asked, it would have been awkward."

"So you killed her?"

"I didn't kill her exactly," he protested. "She was making too much noise. I put my hand over her mouth, and before I knew it she went limp. I didn't know she had a bad heart. I just thought she was nuts, carrying her husband's ashes around with her like that. She said Rita had told you all about it, so of course I had to watch you. And when I saw you take the note out of the compost pile, of course I knew she'd told the truth about that anyway, that you did know."

"I don't know. I know nothing. I was admiring your compost maker and wanted to take a look at it. That's all."

"You read the note. You know about the disks." He shook me, hard. My head wobbled on my neck. "You'll tell Emery, and he'll tell the others. I'd go to jail. That's not okay with me." My vision cleared, and I saw that he was smiling. "I'd rather go to South America."

"Go ahead. I won't stop you."

His smile broadened. "No, you won't."

"Just leave, right now. I won't say anything to anyone."

"Too risky." He pulled me again, hauling me over to the fence. I looked around frantically, hoping to see Amy, Bruno, Tamiko, anyone who could help me. The garden was placid, unruffled by any other humans.

With my head turned toward the library, I must have been in the perfect position for Webster's fist to take me out. I didn't really feel the blow then. All I knew was blackness.

# 25

I came awake with pain radiating through my head from a sore place behind my left ear. I was fighting for breath while Webster stuffed my mouth with something rough and wadded-up—one of his leather gloves. He loomed over me, pushing me down as he worked to knot a bandanna—my own bandanna—around my head to hold the glove in place. I tried to bring my hands up to rip the bandanna off, but they had been tightly secured behind me with what felt like wire. The surface beneath me was mostly spongy, except for the hard, flat object directly under my hipbone. I kicked out and he forced my knees up to my chest and tied the sleeves of Amy's jean jacket tight behind me, trapping my legs like a strait-jacket. I feared that my vision had been affected by the clout on the head he'd given me, because he was framed in a dark circle as he bent over me, as if in an old-fashioned vignette.

Then I noticed the richly smelly aroma that surrounded me. Webster had tossed me into his compost bin, trussed up like a grocery-store turkey waiting for Thanksgiving.

He stepped back a pace, and more of the sky came into view behind his head. "Just lie still," he said in a rough whisper. "You don't want anything bad to happen to anyone else."

He clapped the lid of the bin on, and I was shut into warm, odoriferous darkness. The leaves and garden debris around my ears rustled with every movement, and even when I didn't move, courtesy of roly-poly bugs and worms. Ventilation slits punctured the sides of the bin, making bars of brightness, but not allowing me to see out.

I still felt stunned from the blow, dizzy and unable to think. But I could hear, if I held still to keep the rustling down. I heard Webster moving around his plot, the clink as he took out some tool. And in the distance, coming closer, I could hear running footsteps, which slowed as they reached the perimeter path.

The footsteps were muted by the sound of Webster shoveling in a regular rhythm, accompanied by occasional grunts. I had the hysterical thought that the bed he was digging, no doubt in the well-mounded French Intensive method, would be my grave.

The footsteps slowed more, walking past the compost bin on the perimeter path, not two feet away from my black plastic prison. I could hear Amy's gasps for breath and Barker panting as if he planned to hyperventilate.

"Do you see her, boy?" The footsteps stopped, then resumed a slow walk. "Babe is here, but I don't see Aunt Liz."

Barker didn't reply. It sounded as if he'd flopped down on the dead grass beside the path. Amy must have looped his leash over one of the fence posts. The garden gate creaked. Her footsteps came down the main path, heading for my garden plot. Webster was still digging.

"Hmm." Straining my ears, I could hear the soft sound she made when she saw my spade stuck in the ground, the bag of potatoes and bucket of tools. Silence for a moment, except for Webster's shovel and the soft thud of earth being rearranged. I hoped Amy was picking up on my thought waves, telling her to go immediately to the library and call Bruno.

"Excuse me." Her clear voice sounded closer, coming from the path at the end of Webster's plot. "Have you seen Liz Sullivan? I know she was here. Did you see her leave?"

"I got here a little while ago and no one has come or left since then, except you." The undercurrent of amusement in Webster's voice as he told her this polite, prevaricating truth made me seethe. "Maybe she went to the Dumpster."

"Maybe." I could hear the uneasiness in Amy's voice. I willed her to leave, to run away.

Webster's shovel ceased cutting into the earth. His feet crunched through the mulch; his voice came from farther away. Closer to Amy.

"Tell you what, why don't we walk over and check it out? I can take my weed bucket and empty it."

"No, thanks." Amy's footsteps retreated. "I'll just get started with the potatoes, and then when my aunt comes back, we'll be closer to leaving."

"Suit yourself." In an agony of anticipation, I waited for Webster to take his weed bucket and go. I was sure I could make enough noise to get Barker's attention, and then I would get Amy's.

But Webster didn't leave. He started digging again, in counterpoint to Amy's work in my plot. The shovels bit into the dirt in out-of-sync tandem, *thunk-thunk, thunk-thunk*.

The tight wire twisted around my wrists was cutting off circulation to my fingers, making them stiff and swollen, like bunches of balloons. I could hear Barker, still panting, probably less than ten feet from the bin. I reached as far behind me as I could. Not just my fingers were painful; every movement made my shoulders scream in agony. I was too close to the garden side of the bin to touch its fence side.

Hoping I wouldn't make enough noise to draw Webster's attention, I tried to slither across the bin. My cheek met something slimy, which stuck there. Finally my swollen fingers brushed against the far wall. I moved my hands as best I could, up, down, in a frustratingly small arc. Nothing. I inched up in a different direction, my fingers questing across the hard plastic of the bin.

At last I felt the edge of a ventilation slit. I stuffed one, two sausagey fingers into it, letting them hang down outside the bin below the edge of the slit. I could feel a breeze move along my skin, so I knew the fingers were visible. I hoped they were smellable, too. I did my feeble best to move them enticingly.

Nothing happened for a long, agonizing moment, while the shovels worked together and I waited for Webster to begin to hurt Amy. The breeze intensified, sweeping my pheromones toward the garden gate—toward Barker's sensitive nose. He was probably picking up other rich smells in the immediate area, so I wasn't sure he'd be able to scent mine.

Then Barker whined, softly, and again more loudly. His whine sounded closer. He was on his feet. I pictured him, straining at the leash, his nose pointed in my direction.

Webster's shovel stopped, then started again. He spoke in a loud voice.

"So, are you visiting your aunt for Thanksgiving?"

"Just for a while." Amy's voice held reserve.

"Aren't you in school?" Webster moved a little farther down his plot. I redoubled the motion of my fingers, afraid that at any moment he would leap on Amy and we'd both be goners.

Barker whined again, and then, bless him, gave voice to his signature noise. It wasn't his danger bark, at least not yet. It was his let-me-go-I've-got-something-to-check-out bark, the one usually caused by squirrels or cats.

"Barker. Stop it. Do you see a squirrel? Do you want to chase a squirrel?" Amy sounded indulgent. "You didn't like the leash all the way here, did you? Want to chase those squirrelies, don't you?"

Barker agreed enthusiastically with the tone of the comments, if not with the content.

"Dogs are supposed to be on a leash in Palo Alto. It's the law." Webster sounded edgy. Amy's footsteps went down the main path. The gate creaked.

"I'll put him back on the leash after he has one dash. It's not like he ever catches them."

Letting Barker off the leash, except in places with lots of running space and no leash laws, was strictly forbidden. But I wasn't going to give Amy a hard time over it. I was going to hug her, assuming we both got out of this with whole skins.

I redoubled my wiggling, ignoring the pain in my fingers. Suddenly Barker's rough tongue was licking them. Tears welled up in my eyes.

"What are you eating? No, boy. Bad dog. Garbage." Amy rattled the leash, but Barker kept licking.

"Get him out of my compost," Webster growled, dropping the matey act.

"He's just found something hanging out of your bin." Amy's voice came closer. "What in the world—wait a minute!"

Webster's shovel struck against something nearby, hard enough to give out a twang and send a jolt through the bin. "What are you trying to do?" Amy, breathless and indignant, was retreating toward the parking lot, from the sound of her voice.

"Stop right where you are."

"Is that—do you have a *gun*?" She was incredulous. Barker abandoned my fingers. I could hear his low growl, deep in his chest. It's the only time he's dangerous, when he lets out that growl.

"Stop or I'll shoot you. And your damned dog."

"What is going on?" Amy sounded more impatient than frightened. "Look, if you try to shoot me, a million people are going to come out of the library and find you."

"Library's not open yet." Webster was unruffled. "Now come back through the gate. Slowly. Don't try anything."

"I don't know anything to try." The gate creaked. "What are you going to do? What's this about?"

"It's about a parcel of meddling busybodies," Webster muttered. Amy might not have heard him. Beside me, Barker's growl went on and on. Maybe Webster thought he was safe because of the fence between him and the dog—the fence only a little higher than my picket fence at home.

"Don't touch me, you creep. I'm pregnant!"

Webster laughed. "So? What's that supposed to mean to me? You're in my way. That's all that matters."

"Let go. Let go—that hurts!"

Barker loosed his most fearsome growl, a horrible slavering thing he usually saves for the mail carrier. The sound went right over the bin as he jumped. I could feel the thud of his landing—at fifty pounds, he's solid.

"Stupid dog." Webster's voice was shaken.

"Don't shoot him! *No!*" Amy screamed.

"Bitch. Call him off! Call him off!"

I strained against the bond of the jean jacket, and the knotted sleeves loosened and gave way. It was hard in the spongy mass to get purchase for my legs and straighten up. I got my shoulders against the lid of the bin and heaved up, knocking it off.

A frightening sight met me. Barker had fastened his jaws deeply into Webster's forearm, rendering the gun he held in that hand useless. Webster was trying to raise his arm, shake Barker off, but a big dog isn't easy to budge. He couldn't turn the gun enough to shoot Barker. In his preoccupation, he'd let go of Amy. She was behind him, yanking his shovel out of the dirt.

Amy swung the shovel, missing Webster's head and back, but landing a good clout on his elbow from behind—probably right on his funny bone. The gun flew out of his hand and landed in among his raspberry canes. If I hadn't erupted out of the compost just then, she might have managed to take him out, and it would all have been over.

"Aunt Liz! My God!" Amy flung the shovel away—it landed in Tamiko's garden—and ran to me. Barker was distracted, too. He still gripped Webster's arm, but his ears were no longer flattened against his head, and his eyes rolled back toward me.

Webster shook his arm again, and this time Barker dropped off. He had broken the skin; blood seeped through the sleeve of Webster's trendy barn jacket.

"Damn you all!" He looked around for the shovel, but it was out of sight among Tamiko's fava beans. Barker lunged at him again, getting him in the thigh.

I held Amy's gaze, unable to talk with the gag in my mouth, and jerked my head toward the library. She nodded and swung one leg over the chicken-wire fence.

Webster lashed out with his other foot at Barker, who yelped and skittered back. "Barker!" Amy swung back around.

Balked of his weapons, Webster spotted the wheelbarrow loaded with heavy bags of soil conditioner. He grabbed the handles, and with a spurt of maniacal strength, drove it in a rush straight at Amy.

Her mouth formed a disbelieving O, her eyes wide. The wheelbarrow rammed into her, mashing her against the chicken-wire fence.

Webster ran across Tamiko's plot, through the gate and out through the trees toward the parking lot. Moments later, an engine roared to life and drove away.

I was frantic, unable to help Amy with my wrists still imprisoned behind me and my mouth stopped with Webster's leather glove. Amy's eyes lost their glazed look, though her face was very white. Slowly she pushed the wheelbarrow away, and then collapsed against the fence. Whining anxiously, Barker licked her face.

"Oh, Barker." She put her arms around his neck and let him drag her toward the compost bin. When she was close enough, she managed to pull herself up the side of it.

"Aunt Liz." Her fingers fumbled with the knot of bandanna, and finally freed me to spit out the noxious glove. "My God. Are you okay?"

"Are you?" I had a hard time forming the words—my mouth was dry and felt misshapen.

"Yeah." She didn't sound okay. She was working now at the wire that held my wrists together. "Your hands. My God."

The bond loosened, and my arms fell to my sides with painful relief. I tried to raise them, to look at my hands, but I couldn't make them work. At the ends of my arms were obscene-looking purple appendages.

"They'll recover." I looked around anxiously. "We've got to call Bruno right away." I put one hand on the edge of the bin to climb out before I realized that wasn't going to work. "Run and call him, use that pay phone. Wait, be careful, make sure Webster's gone before you go."

Amy didn't move. She leaned against the bin, and then slowly slid down until she was sitting on the ground. "I can't," she whispered. "Something is wrong. You'll have to go, Aunt Liz."

I managed to sit on the edge of the bin next to the fence, swing my legs over, get down on the other side of the fence without falling. I have no clear recollection of how I managed to find a coin in my pocket and use the pay phone.

My fingers were still bloated when the ambulance arrived minutes later. By the time Bruno got there, as the EMTs were putting Amy into the ambulance, the tingling in my hands was intensifying into exquisite pain, a good sign, one of the EMTs told me.

"You get in there, too." Bruno wouldn't take no for an answer, and I didn't want to leave Amy anyway. He put

Barker in his car and followed us in the ambulance. I held her hand in one of my throbbing ones and watched her grow paler and paler.

At the hospital, an intern examined the lump on my head and my lacerated wrists with great interest, assuring me I'd live and be healed up in no time. A nurse sponged off my face and hands, getting an incredibly dirty basin of water in return. I noticed that people wrinkled up their noses when they first came within sniffing distance of my redolent atmosphere. Bruno and I had a large clear space around us in the waiting room while I told him what had happened and we waited to learn how Amy was.

"Thanks, by the way." I smiled at him, glad it was Bruno who sat with me in my unlovely state, and not Drake.

"For what?" He was polite enough not to hold his nose while we talked. His laptop had received much information, and he'd made several calls on his cell phone, while we waited.

"For getting them to treat Amy without insisting on calling her parents. They'll have to know about the attack, but maybe they won't have to know about—the rest of it."

"Do you not think she'll tell them?"

"She might. But I sure wouldn't in her place." It was going to be bad enough to tell them about what she'd gone through in the garden.

He looked at me with great sympathy. "She will lose the baby, you know."

"I guessed as much." I didn't know how she would take this abrupt ending to her dilemma, whether with relief or sadness. "As long as there's no permanent damage."

"We will hope that is so."

I shifted position, trying to balance the tub of ice that the nurse had insisted I keep my hands immersed in, and heard a crackling in the front pocket of my overalls. "Oh, there's that." I indicated the pocket with my chin. "Can you get that, Bruno?" It was the sealed plastic bag, which I'd tucked away before the ambulance had arrived.

Bruno examined it with interest. "And it was Emery he mentioned?"

"He thought I'd tell Emery, which would be bad for Webster." I didn't want Bruno to get the wrong idea. "It must have to do with industrial espionage. Emery had a patch of that not too long ago. I guess Webster was involved, and with some of the other companies he worked for, too. The only thing that puzzles me is why he'd use the garden as a drop spot. Why not just copy everything electronically and send it along?"

"Those transmissions are easier to trace than you might think." Bruno looked up from the screen. "But the garden was a stupid choice. An arrogant choice, rather. Mr. Powell liked thinking that everything fell into his plans. But sooner or later at a place like the garden, someone was bound to notice something."

"Rita must have." I lifted my hands from the ice, letting them drip. "I'll get frostbite if I keep this up."

Bruno didn't pay attention. "Rita actually went out with him for a while, didn't she?"

I nodded. "Somehow she figured out what he was up to. Maybe he even said something, bragged about his secret life. I don't think he could keep things to himself, not when they showed how clever he was."

"You are probably right." Bruno took out his cell

phone again and dialed. "Did you find him?" He listened, and after a moment said, "Well, keep on it. We may have to enlarge the perimeter. And make sure they are staying on it at the airports and emergency rooms."

"He said something about South America to me."

Bruno passed that along and then put the cell phone away.

A doctor came purposefully toward us. "Ms. Sullivan?" He ignored Bruno, who typed away on his keyboard. "Your niece is asking for you."

I abandoned the tub of ice thankfully, and he led me away. Bruno walked with us through the corridors. They had admitted Amy to a room—a double, not a ward, and the other bed was unoccupied. Bruno stepped back so I could go through the door alone, though I noticed he left it ajar.

Amy was propped up in the bed, wearing a hospital gown, the covers pulled up around her waist. "Did you hear?" She blinked at me, her eyes moist. "I lost the baby."

"I heard." I went up to the bed and put an arm around her shoulders. "I'm so sorry, honey."

"I'm not." Amy sat up straighter. "I feel like a creep for that, but I'm glad. The doctor said the fetus had a problem anyway—" She thought for a moment. "A neural tube defect, I think it was. Otherwise, I probably wouldn't have miscarried, even with major gut trauma."

"Poor Amy."

She waved off my sympathy; her thoughts were still on the baby. "It could never have lived long. I would have gone through all that, torn my family up, just to provide some childless people with a baby, and then the baby wouldn't have been the kind anyone wanted." She slumped back. "It's dumb to do things for other people's reasons. You should figure out your own reasons and do what's best for you."

"That would work most of the time."

She didn't really hear me. "I don't mind the pain so much, because it's reminding me never to be so stupid again."

"Will you be able to have children later?"

"They did MRIs and stuff, and they said nothing was permanently injured, just bruised. Because the fence behind me gave, you see. If I'd been up against a wall or something, I might have really gotten hurt." She sniffled into a tissue. "The way I feel right now, I'm going on the pill and never going off. This isn't a good world for babies. What was it about, Aunt Liz? Why did that guy have to rupture my guts?"

Bruno came in. "I will answer your questions, Miss Amy, but first, are you able to answer a few of mine?"

Amy asserted that she was suffering more from curiosity than anything else. A nurse brought her a little white paper cup of meds and she swallowed them down without question. I wondered how much pain medicine she had already gotten, and how long she'd have to be in the hospital. And how I was going to pay for it.

I sat in the chair by the window, half listening to Bruno's questions and Amy's answers. I would have to call the senior center and tell them I couldn't do the workshop that day. I would stay with Amy until she succumbed to her medication, and then I could go home. I could smear a liberal amount of comfrey salve on my

221

abraded wrists, get together some home comforts to take back to the hospital for Amy, and give thanks that we were both alive.

# 26

"SO Webster was behind that contract we lost a few months ago." Emery was still stunned, even though a full day had passed since Bruno had spoken to him. "I didn't even think of him. I figured it was some hacker lifting our files, not someone I knew."

"Your company wasn't the only one." I scrubbed the radishes and sliced them into long ovals for the salad I was composing.

Bridget pulled a couple of big pans of lasagna out of the oven, and put in several foil-wrapped loaves of garlic bread. "If I had a double oven," she muttered, "the lasagna wouldn't get cold while the garlic bread cooked."

"Maybe my company will do better now that Webster's been arrested, and we'll finally be able to remodel." Emery popped the top off his beer bottle. The hum of conversation from the living room was punctuated with frequent laughter. Claudia's deep voice boomed, telling a joke. She'd been properly "surprised" by finding a living room full of friends, instead of Emery and Bridget ready to leave her with their children. I had been glad to escape all the hearty conviviality to help finish dinner preparations in the kitchen.

"So where did they find him?" Bridget threw the

question over her shoulder while she dove into a drawer for aluminum foil.

"Waiting with his arm in a sling at the San Francisco airport for a plane to South America. It turns out he has another identity already established on an island off the Venezuelan coast. They think they can recover some of the money. You should put in a claim, Emery."

"Make it enough to remodel the kitchen," Bridget said. "How's Amy doing?"

"She's better." I fell silent, washing cherry and golden pear tomatoes. Amy was physically okay. She'd been discharged from the hospital with a supply of sanitary pads and instructions to take it easy. I had given her my bed for the duration, and she was no doubt immured there with her headphones and CD player, her stack of CDs— and Jane Austen's *Emma*, which she'd expressed an interest in reading after finding it on my shelves.

It grieved me to see the dimming of her sparkle, the bruised look around her eyes. With time, she could surely get back that self-confident trust in her own abilities and in the world's recognition of them. I hoped she hadn't gone too far along the road that leads to closing off parts of yourself to avoid hurt. Those doors are the devil to open up again.

"No lasting troubles?"

"All systems will be go, the doctors said. Not that Amy wants them to go. She's swearing eternal chastity."

"That won't last long." Bridget covered the tops of the lasagna pans with foil. "The salad looks beautiful."

"Thanks." I regarded it with pride. Melanie would have no occasion to find me coming up short that night. I scattered the *pièce de résistance* on top—gold and orange and red nasturtiums, pink and white carnation petals, tiny white flowers culled from the bolting stems of my parsley, small blue stars of rosemary.

"A work of art." Bridget shook up the jar of vinaigrette I'd brought and took a whiff. "This smells divine, too, though it's almost a shame to put dressing on that."

Melanie came in the back door, casually elegant in flowing pants and shirt, carrying a huge pink box from the Prolific Oven. "Sorry I'm late. Where can I put this? Is Claudia here yet?"

"You missed the surprise." Bridget took the cake box and put it on the table. "Everyone's in the other room. We're just getting ready to serve."

Melanie looked over the table, which had been extended with all its leaves into a long oval. It was set up like a buffet with plates, napkins, glasses, and a couple of big bottles of wine.

"Very nice," Melanie said. "Lovely flowers."

"Liz brought them." Bridget leaned over the table for a long whiff of a half-open Margaret Merrill. "Aren't they divine? Such perfume."

"I must get you to talk to my gardener, Liz. All I have is a few pansies and some impatiens." Melanie glanced through the kitchen door at the swarm of people in the living room, and then at the table again. "Did you need me to bring plates?"

"Not at all." Bridget smiled blandly. "We're using paper."

"I would have been glad to have the party at my house, you know, if only things weren't so uncertain with Hugh."

"You're doing enough by providing me with a baby-sitter. And I don't mind paper." Bridget winked at me. "Or plastic forks."

I intervened before Melanie could have an apoplexy.

"There is no plastic, and Bridget has plenty of plates, and I'm sure you'll be glad to stay after and help wash up, right, Melanie?"

"If there's time." She frowned at me. "By the way, what's this story I hear about you getting involved with counterfeiting?"

"Honestly, the things people will make up." Bridget leaped to my defense, which I always found agreeable. "There's no truth to that at all, Melanie. There were no counterfeiters. I don't know how this kind of thing gets started. Only those deaths in the garden, and they didn't involve Liz any more than they did your high-school crush, Tom Dancey."

Melanie clicked her tongue. "Poor Tom has gone on vacation. That's what his brother told my neighbor's bridge partner. Dancey Construction is redoing her house, and Tom was supposed to schedule the finish work, but he's off for a while."

"Rita's death really was a shock for him."

"That's what my neighbor said. She said everyone knew they were lovers for a while."

"It's sad." Bridget's mind was elsewhere. "Emery, should we open the wine now?"

"Only if we're ready to eat." Emery looked through the kitchen door. "It'll all be gone before we even get food on our plates if you open it too soon. The snacks are almost done for as it is. The cheese is just a memory."

"I believe we are ready to eat, if Liz will dress the salad. The garlic bread's hot, and I've got more wine hidden in the pantry. So let 'er rip."

"Shouldn't we pull the table out more into the middle of the room?" Unable to resist meddling, Melanie grabbed one end of the table. Bridget, perforce, took the other end. "And let's bring the lasagna over—just one, we'll leave the other one on the stove."

"Good idea." Bridget didn't appear to resent Melanie taking over her party.

Melanie peeled the foil off one of the pans of lasagna. "Shouldn't we cut this now? And has Liz tossed the salad?" She looked over at me and squealed. "What happened to your hands?"

"A gardening accident." The lacerations around my wrists had responded nicely to the herbal salve. My hands were still a little swollen, and dark with bruising. Melanie shuddered and looked away.

Claudia came into the kitchen, followed by other party-goers. "What lovely flowers!" She made a beeline for the roses, which Bridget had arranged with sea lavender in an old silver urn. "From your garden, Liz. I recognize our favorite Oklahoma." She nodded majestically at the salad. "Very pretty. And I understand people do actually eat the flowers."

Bridget smothered a smile. People crowded around the table, exclaiming at the savory odors. Melanie took the top off the cake box with a flourish, revealing a rich-looking chocolate sheet cake emblazoned, in white, HAPPY 60TH BIRTHDAY, CLAUDIA!

Claudia froze. The noise died down. Even Melanie felt the change in the atmosphere and fell back a pace.

"How unfortunate." When she spoke, Claudia's voice sounded almost normal. "Someone has made a mistake in my age."

Melanie was made of stern stuff, but even she quailed. "I'm sorry, Claudia. Did I make a *faux pas*? I just didn't think—"

"No, I'm gratified, my dear." Claudia gave Melanie a cold smile. "But you didn't get it right. I'm sixty-one."

Someone laughed, and then everyone was laughing. Claudia caught my eye sternly, and I shrugged. She couldn't really have thought that I or anyone else had any influence over Melanie.

The food was delicious. I stood around Bridget's kitchen with the rest of the party-goers, eating and listening to the swirl of conversation, immersed in the indiscriminate human warmth. Lois and Rita were dead; Webster was deprived of liberty. Amy was wounded, body and spirit, and I had only to look at my hands to realize that mortality lies in wait for us at any given moment.

Bridget finished guiding people around the food. With her own plate, she came to stand by me. "What's the latest with Drake, anyway? How's his dad?"

"I don't know. He didn't call last night. But the day before, they'd done a bone marrow transplant, which caused some kind of medical crisis, so it could be hectic today. I hope everything's all right." I wanted badly to talk to Paul, to tell him about the whole experience, have him absolve me of wrong choices, of putting Amy in danger through my own stupidity. I wanted to believe that I deserved absolution for that, since I was going to have to call Renee and Andy soon. Amy had begged to put it off until she felt stronger, and since the hospital had written me down as her guardian, Renee and Andy hadn't been notified of the incident. They deserved to know that their child had been injured; in their places I'd want to know. But in this, as in everything else, I was trying to get out of Amy's way and let her make her own decisions. Such a policy might be totally stupid, as Renee would no doubt see it, but it was the only one I had.

"Is Amy still planning to stay with you?"

"No." I couldn't confess, even to a forgiving person like Bridget, how relieved I was by Amy's decision to go back home at the end of her allotted stay. "She's going to go ahead and use her return ticket, so she'll be leaving in just over a week."

"Time to do some college visiting, after all."

"If she's up to it."

"She will be. She's young and resilient. She'll learn the lesson and forget the terror."

"I hope so. I feel terribly guilty, like I let her get into trouble."

"You had nothing to do with it." Bridget noticed someone trying to pour wine from an empty bottle. "Excuse me. I'm going to get out the reserves."

Claudia tapped her fork on her wineglass. It was time for the witty speech extempore, I supposed.

"Thank you all," she said into the fresh quiet. "It is very nice of you to remember my birthday, although I wish some of you had remembered which one it is less well." She looked at Melanie, who gave a coy wave.

"However, something more important than my birthday happened today." Claudia pulled a piece of paper out of her pocket—a page torn from a magazine. "I opened up *Publishers Weekly*, and found a review of Bridget's first novel."

Everyone exclaimed. Bridget, emerging from the party with a bottle of wine under each arm, looked incredulous.

"It's not even supposed to be out until January."

"Reviewers are sent advance copies," Claudia said, dismissing this with a wave of the paper. "This review is not simply good—it positively raves. 'A luminous narrative,' it says. 'Montrose authentically captures the inner life of her characters.' 'A perfect achievement.' It is a starred review, much coveted by authors. I congratulate Biddy. Here's to seeing her book on the best-seller list!"

Emery gave Bridget a big hug and took away the bottles of wine before she lost her grip on them. Claudia thrust the review into her hands, and she began to read it, her face still wearing an expression of utter astonishment.

"Well, looks like Bridget might be able to pay for remodeling the kitchen," Emery said, pulling the cork out of one bottle. "I'll drink to that."

It was wonderful seeing Bridget so overwhelmed by her good fortune. I watched the energy of the party swirl between her and Claudia while I finished my salad. The carnation petals transformed their fragrance into the taste of vanilla in my mouth, and the peppery nasturtiums were like a series of tiny flavor explosions. I thought about the harvest I'd reap from the raised beds the next day, and the seed potatoes still waiting for me at the garden. I thought about Drake coming back from Seattle, about opening some of those doors I'd closed so many years ago.

It was almost eight o'clock. I gave Claudia a hug, and another one to Bridget, with whispered congratulations. We would talk about it all later, at the garden or in my kitchen or hers, without so many half-drunk poets around.

Then I set out into the damp, chilly night to walk the two blocks to my house—Drake's house—and wait beside his telephone.

I had a lot to say to him.

*Don't miss the earlier Liz Sullivan mysteries!*

# MURDER IN A NICE NEIGHBORHOOD
## by Lora Roberts

While vagabond writer Liz Sullivan lies innocently sleeping in her '69 VW microbus, someone parks a dead body under it. The victim was a vagrant with whom Liz shared some unpleasant words just hours before the murder.

Setup? Maybe. But the police figure they've got their woman—unless Liz can provide them with a better alternative....

Published by Fawcett Books.
Available at your local bookstore.

# MURDER IN THE MARKETPLACE
## by Lora Roberts

Freelance writer Liz Sullivan is on the scene when the body of beautiful Jenifer Paston is discovered. Jenifer happened to be a star at SoftWrite, the Silicon Valley company where Liz is temping.

Unfortunately, freelance writing doesn't pay the bills—so Liz is forced to continue working at SoftWrite, where spite, sex, and greed take top priority, and where the computer games are murder.

# MURDER MILE HIGH

## by Lora Roberts

For the first time in years, struggling writer Liz Sullivan is headed home to Denver to visit her estranged family. No sooner does she arrive than her former husband's corpse is delivered to her father's front porch with a bullet between the eyes.

Since Liz once tried to kill her violently abusive husband, the police assume she has finally succeeded....

# MURDER
# BONE BY BONE
## by Lora Roberts

Liz Sullivan is astonished when the two boys she is baby-sitting dig up human bones from the sidewalk under construction in front of their house.

Whose bones? Positive identification seems unlikely, but they appear to have been stashed away some thirty years ago. Liz and her friend police detective Paul Drake begin to ask questions—and they resurrect a past that will drive someone to murder in order to keep buried.

Published by Fawcett Books.
Available at your local bookstore.